AMOR FATI

Jack Smith

Jack Smith's latest novel, AMOR FATI, told mostly in brilliant dialogue, is brisk, farcical and disturbing. His self-apologetic teen-aged, and relatively privileged male protagonist acts on wishful fantasies of lust, love, and material success, but as the teen's mistakes grow dumb and dumber, the reader is held in a limbo of sympathy. After all, Smith implies, surrounded by vapid peers and corrupt predators—prostitutes, mobsters, lawyers, judges—what passes for fate amounts to social conditioning. Farce morphs into Kafkaesque comedy, then Westian satire.

DeWitt Henry
Author of THE MARRIAGE OF ANNA MAYE POTTS and TOP COP KILLS

In this satirical amalgam of good and evil, Jack Smith has welded together a story of Love, Law, The Mob, Comparison Shopping, Money, Hit Men, and Impetuous Youth. Frederick lives on the edge but wants to live like a prince with Lilac, his princess, and his red sports car. But life isn't easy for a boy on the outside and when the Law gets him by the throat, his life takes a left turn. Pay up or it's prison, son. Look at this tale as a tour de force rich with dialogue, character, action, and think "the deep belly laugh of the cosmic guffaw." Nothing is sacred in this modern-day Romeo and Juliet with an urban twist. Yes, love does find a way but not the way you'd expect. Great fun. A fast read.

Jack Remick
Author of MAN ALONE, GABRIELA AND THE WIDOW, BLOOD, THE CALIFORNIA QUARTET, and CITADEL

In the midst of his own life's mess, Hamlet moans, "How all occasions do inform against me." He didn't know the half of it compared with the lot of teenage Frederick. For every attempt to climb out of a hole, the boy's fate digs him in deeper—confronted by thugs with tire irons, a corrupt judge, a gun toting gangster, loan sharks, a desperate father, and a toying girl who demands more and more. His lawyer, Edmund Bulge, knows what Frederick faces: "Well, then, son, You're in a peck of trouble. You're what they call screwed." Mr. Dark underlines that "We're stuck with the hand we're dealt." An apartment manager urges him to "Love his fate." Frederick's capacity for such affection is certainly tested. Can he bring himself to embrace all of the woes Jack Smith heaps upon him?

Walter Cummins
Author of SEEKING AUTHENTICITY

Jack Smith does it again with Amor Fati: an uncommon premise, snappy and engaging dialogue, quirkiness and oddity that will keep you both smiling and turning pages. Read this book!

Mark Wish
Pushcart-Prize-Winning author
of NECESSARY DEEDS

The narrative of Jack Smith's AMOR FATI doesn't move so much on a straight line as it does on a wheel of fate with the spokes of love spinning this tale down avenues of escalating chaos. It's a trenchant attack on the American Dream, emphasizing the dark side of debts and loans and more debts and loans. And as always, Smith's trademark dialogue is crisp, original, and full of comical non-sequiturs and zingers. An absolute hoot!

Grant Tracey
Author of the **HAYDEN FULLER MYSTERY SERIES**
and Editor, *North American Review*

The trajectory of a young man's life changes in an instant when he throws an ill-fated punch, setting into motion a chain of events that draws him further and further into a spiraling future. Jack Smith's witty, engaging, and thought-provoking AMOR FATI reveals how what we do shapes our future, and how much of our lives can hinge on a particular moment.

Midge Raymond
Author of **FLOREANA** and **MY LAST CONTINENT**

If Raymond Carver and Elmore Leonard had a love child, Jack Smith would be it. In AMOR FATI, Smith has given his fans a darkly comic novel, the dialogue and action breakneck, the questionable decisions accruing with an inevitability that makes it impossible to stop turning the pages.

Christine Sneed
Author of THE VIRGINITY OF FAMOUS MEN
and PLEASE BE ADVISED: A NOVEL IN MEMOS

First printing, 14 February 2025
Library of Congress Control Number: 2024942667
ISBN 978-1-953136-85-5 Hardback
ISBN 978-1-953136-86-2 Paperback

Cover Design by Kurt Lovelace
Cover Artwork by Pierian Springs Press
Cover type *Bauhaus Dessau* **Alfarn** by Céline Hurka,
Elia Preuss, Flavia Zimbardi,
Hidetaka Yamasaki, and Luca Pellegrini.
Body & Chapter Titles set in **No 9T**
Headers in **Jenson** by Robert Slimbach
Flourishes set in Emigre Foundry **Dalliance**, by Frank Heine
&
Emigre Foundry **ZeitGuys**, by Bob Aufuldish, Eric Donelan.
Typefaces licensed Adobe, Linotype, Emigre, & URW GmbH.

PSPress.Pub
Pierian Springs Press, Inc
30 N Gould St, Ste 25398
Sheridan, Wyoming 82801-6317

To
Mary Jane Smith

CONTENTS

Introduction by Jack Remick

Chapter 1 | 1
Chapter 2 | 13
Chapter 3 | 21
Chapter 4 | 31
Chapter 5 | 39
Chapter 6 | 53
Chapter 7 | 61
Chapter 8 | 71
Chapter 9 | 77
Chapter 10 | 85
Chapter 11 | 95
Chapter 12 | 103
Chapter 13 | 111
Chapter 14 | 119
Chapter 15 | 123
Chapter 16 | 135
Chapter 17 | 145
Chapter 18 | 155
Chapter 19 | 159
Chapter 20 | 163
Chapter 21 | 171

ACKNOWLEDGMENTS | 181

ABOUT THE AUTHOR | 182

ALSO BY JACK SMITH | 184

Introduction to *Amor Fati*

Jack Remick

Novelists now live, like it or not, in an Age of Images. An age shaped by the screen and directed by the moving image codified in the ninety-minute screenplay repeated with gusto throughout the creative world of the small screen—television and the Big Screen—Movies. Running on a hundred languages, fueled by money, the screenplay and its final product, the moving image, has not only redefined the Highest form of art but it has rewired our brains. Not an easy task given the precursors of High Art such as Richard Wagner, the Italian composers and the titans of Broadway who brought the novel to life and, on stage, set the stage for an evolution unlike any since the first pictures gracing the walls of Chauvet. Art, no matter how you look at it, has been on a single-minded evolutionary track, for at least thirty-thousand years, to make images move. The modern mind no longer finds satisfaction in the static art of the past. No, the modern mind, reshaped by the genius of film, demands motion. In one phase of the evolution, we do see attempts at movement—Hindu sculpture, Baroque excess, Calder mobiles—but it took film—first film and the screenplay to reshape the nature and impulse of writing. In sum, the moving image has us reshape and remake the novel.

In Jack Smith's satirical piece, *Amor Fati*, we see the elements of the screenplay in embryo—action sequences, image strings, focused images, fast-running dialogue, and that quintessential filmic reality—the action-image.

He was drunk when he got in his father's second car, a dull green piece of junk. As he drove, he closed one eye to be sure he could see the oncoming traffic. He almost ran a red light, but got through the intersection, half of it anyway, just as the yellow was turning red.

Fast Running Dialogue:

At first he stood a few feet away from that doorway. And then he moved forward, step by step. He peeked in. A woman was looking down at Horatio Dark lying there. She was fondling his hair. She was smiling, or half smiling, and humming something to herself. And then she began singing a tune of some sort. It sounded like a lullaby. And then she looked up and spotted him.

"Yes? Did you want something?"

"I got the wrong room."

She glared at him. "No, you didn't. You got the right room. You're that bad boy, aren't you? That one."

He looked at her, then looked quickly away at some sort of machine with green lights blinking. Then he looked back. "Which boy?"

"Don't play games with me. I've talked to the police, young man. I know who you are and I saw your face in the yearbook. A big smile. You're not smiling now, are you? You feeling guilty? Is that it? For killing my poor little boy?"

"Killing?" he said.

"I'd think you would. Look at my poor son, lying like this. Dead to the world. Just dead. Dead."

"Dead?"

"He might as well be."

She might be about to cry, but she just gently stroked

Horatio Dark's hair. And then she seemed to become absorbed by something, some thought, something. He watched her for a few long minutes. Had she fainted?

"I'm sorry. I didn't mean to. It just sort of... happened."

"Sure," came her voice. "Sure."

He started to leave.

"Come here. Step this way."

"What? What do you—"

"I need help moving him."

What we see, in *Amor Fati*, is the screenplay rendered in fictional, narrative format. What's missing is the scene format that all films must—there is no choice, there is no second best—adhere to. *Amor Fati* is, no matter how you look at it, a novel waiting for its screenwriter to transfer it to that scene format.

In *Amor Fati*, Jack Smith gives us Scene Shifts:

And there, at that party, Horatio Dark had stood by, lounging against the wall with a drink of whiskey and had said casually.

"Lilac? What the hell kind of name is that? I had to laugh the first time I heard it. But in bed, what a tigress. Huh?"

"What?" ... "What did you say?"

"In bed. You need that repeated, do you?"

"You bastard," said Frederick.

"She's a bitch," said Dark, smirking. "A cute little bitch. But a bitch all the same."

And that's when he'd hauled off and let him have it, right on the chin.

He thought he heard bones snapping.

And that's when, a second later, the man toppled over. In that regard, though, Frederick was lucky be-cause a few guys standing next to Dark caught the bastard before he landed on his head.

"Help him up," yelled one of them.

"I'm calling 911," said Frederick.

And he did.

Jack Smith gives us Location Shifts:

He'd found a second-floor apartment with an outside entrance. The old lady who rented it made him put down a deposit of one hundred and seventy-five with the first month's rent due as soon as he moved in. He had six hundred still in his account from some odd jobs he'd picked up, including janitorial work on weekends at the school, and summers, and that would pretty much clean him out.

That apartment. He could bring in girls with that out-side entrance. It was to the back of the house, and you had to walk up a flight of rickety wooden steps, but it was safe. The thing was, there was to be no member of the opposite sex allowed.

"I run a respectable house," the old woman had said. "And I do hear. If I hear a young lady up there laughing or carrying on, that'll be that."

The pieces are here, in *Amor Fati*, just one transition away from a full-scale, ironic, satirical take on America and the hidden themes that make the nation ripe for satire: Love, Law, The Mob, Comparison Shopping, Money, Hit Men, Perpetual, Impetuous, Never-aging Youth. And cars. Cars. Cars. Nothing is sacred in this modern-day Romeo and Juliet with an urban twist. As so many of us say after we finish an ink and paper novel--"This would make one hell of a movie..."

Jack Remick

AMOR FATI

1

In a half hour his lawyer was to arrive, and they'd have a few minutes to confer. It was his father's lawyer, not his. He couldn't afford a lawyer, and he'd never needed one. Until now. Now he did. Or at least they told him he did.

His lawyer's name was Edmund Bulge. He had a bulging stomach in that tight beige sweater, and that affected Frederick's view of him; he couldn't get that bulge out of his mind. Even as the man talked, it seemed to distract him, interfering with his listening.

It was a simple matter, he told Bulge. He had struck this guy named Horatio—yes, that was his real name—and the young man—older than himself, though—had collapsed as soon as his fist connected with his chin. He'd called 911 himself, and the ambulance had arrived. He'd gone in the ambulance with this Horatio... Dark was his last name—yes, that was actually his name. Horatio Dark. He'd stayed with him all the way to the Emergency Room. The doctor had gotten his story, then called the cops. And here he was. Here, right here, and he needed help. It looked like this Horatio... he would be okay. According to the doctor, anyway, and he ought to know. But he'd broken the law and he needed help. Since Mr. Bulge was his father's lawyer, he was hoping he might help him. He had tried to act honorably. Hadn't he?

"I've spoken to your father. He's on his way," said Bulge.

"Do I—do I have a chance?"

"Why'd you do it?"

"He offended me."

"How's that?"

"Called my girlfriend a bitch."

"Um. This Horatio Dark—he's not a man to fool with." Bulge shook his head.

"Huh?"

The cop who'd arrested him poked his head in the doorway.

"Just a moment," said Bulge. "We're not quite finished here."

"Finish up soon," said the cop. He swung out into the hall, and Bulge stood up and went to the door and shut it.

"What can I do?" asked Frederick.

"Did he threaten you? Did he start it—physically, I mean?"

Should he lie? He was not good at lying. "I don't think so."

"You don't think so? You surely know, don't you?"

Three inches of snow on the ground, frozen spots on the sidewalks, a bank of snow against the curbs. It was a cold, cold night, and it seemed merciless with that icy wind. "I didn't like the way he stood there. He's big, you know. And imposing. That's the right word. And I guess... I suppose I just... panicked."

"Um."

"You know?"

Mr. Bulge nodded. And then he scratched his bearded chin. "That happens, I suppose, but in this world you've got to control urges. Urges like that. God only knows we've all had them. We've all wanted to slam a man down and get on him and throttle him but good. We've all felt like that, and on occasion we've come close to it. But then something grips us right by the shoulder blades and says, 'Get a grip, now. Don't do that.' And so we don't. Not all the way anyway." His eyes were focused on Frederick's like he had latched hold of them somehow. "But you did."

"Am I going to jail? Am I?"

Suddenly, in the doorway his father appeared. He was a man of fifty, wearing a gray wool coat and matching scarf. He was brushing off snow. It was feathering his gray hair.

The cop showed up again, right behind him.

"Just a moment, with my son," said his father. "It won't take long."

"We must proceed soon," said the cop.

"It won't take long at all," said his father. He was a patient man. He sat down next to Bulge, directly across from Frederick. "You hit a man?"

"My age," said Frederick. "Older... by a few years. Just a few."

"Well, a man, then, isn't he?"

"Yes, sir."

He had to go over the whole thing again, and he was tired of it. He could've gotten on top of Horatio Dark and beaten his face in, but he'd restrained himself, he pointed out.

"Dark? No one has a name like that," said his father. "And no one has the name of Horatio." He turned to Bulge. "Do they?"

"This one does."

"It's most unusual," said his father.

He'd heard him say things like that when he was

speaking of a real estate deal. When he thought the price wasn't right, either not enough or too much. Most unusual. He was a thoughtful man. He would never hit another man. He would undoubtedly try to make him see his point of view. He would undoubtedly try to reason with him and then when that failed, he'd offer his hand for a shake. A most unusual man, thought Frederick.

"Don't say a thing," said his father. "Your attorney, Mr. Bulge here, will do the talking. Unless, of course, he thinks you should speak. And then do speak. Understood?"

"Yes, sir," said Frederick.

"Good."

The cop stuck his face in the door.

"We're ready now," said Bulge.

"Come in," said his father and extended his hand.

The cop took it, but it was clear he didn't want to shake it. It was so brief, it really wasn't a handshake at all.

❦ ❦ ❦

He'd have to appear in court in a few weeks, on a Friday, when his algebra test was scheduled, which meant, of course, getting an excuse. "Of course that could change," said Bulge, "depending on the judge's pleasure."

"What do you mean?"

"What? On what the judge is wanting, doing, fomenting for."

"Oh."

He debated it. Surely a court appearance would be an excuse, unless his teacher thought that assault and battery wouldn't do and he should pay for it in more ways than one, suffering in his grade as well as in other ways.

He'd gone out to see Horatio Dark, which his father recommended since it showed concern, and judges just loved that, said Bulge. "It shows fellow feeling." Bulge banged his chest. "Preparatory, you see, to heartfelt compunction. Ah!"

The man lay there in bed gripping his Geography text with mammoth hands.

Like him, the young man was a senior, though Dark had repeated his last year a few times. He was set to graduate in May, as was Frederick.

Frederick approached Dark in his bed. He said, "I didn't mean... sorry, I mean. Sorry." Then he extended his hand for a shake, but there was no hand to shake. He tried to make small talk, and then Dark said, "This won't help, you know. I'm pressing charges. To the fullest extent of the law."

"Um," said Frederick. "I really—"

"You really what?"

"I really wish you wouldn't."

Dark fingered his olive complexion. Then he grinned. "We don't always get what we want. Now do we?"

And that was that, and he left. He would not cower before Horatio Dark. He would not be a suck-up.

❧ ❧ ❧

He had just cold-cocked a man bigger than him, and to his mind that was enough: he should be able to drink. And not just on the sly either, but at a bar. Right there as big as you please. He looked older, didn't he? Some said he looked like he was twenty-one. One guy said he looked twenty-three. He could pass for twenty-three, really, especially with that five-o'clock shadow.

"But get you an ID," he was told. "That'll fix you up, at

least with the bars—watch out for the cops, though. They don't like that one bit."

This guy was nineteen himself, in his first year of college, and he'd been drinking at bars since he was sixteen, he told Frederick.

The guy's name was Bell. Ernest or something like that. He didn't quite catch it in all the noise in that bar. He was of medium height, had a beard, and smoked constantly, lighting one off the other. Frederick didn't like to be in range of that. Second-hand smoke. It could kill you. Of course that would be many, many years down the road when he was fifty, sixty, seventy, or even eighty. Still, who wanted to die like that, with your lungs black and rotting. He'd seen the pictures. In Health class, they had some bad ones. Looked like burnt meat. He'd seen good examples of that when his father was barbecuing.

Still, he put all that aside and smoked one whenever he got a chance with Bell, who was a great conversationalist.

This evening, Bell wanted to know more about what had been circulating around. He'd missed that party. Had Frederick actually cold-cocked Dark?

Frederick nodded. He motioned his beer at the bartender. The bartender was a young guy who didn't seem to care about much of anything. Other than the football game on five different monitors.

"Yes—I did. I got him but good."

"Tough guy."

"Well, he pissed me off. You know?"

Bell laughed. "He's in the hospital, is he?"

"Two days now—going on."

"You finished him off good, huh?"

"Yeah. But the law's on my case."

"Get the wrong judge and you'll do time. Thought of that?"

Frederick swallowed. "I've got a good lawyer."

"Maybe that'll help. Could. But who knows?"

﹡﹡﹡

He was drunk when he got in his father's second car, a dull green piece of junk. As he drove, he closed one eye to be sure he could see the oncoming traffic. He almost ran a red light, but got through the intersection, half of it anyway, just as the yellow was turning red.

At home, he went straight up to his room.

Three light knocks. That was his father.

"Come in."

His father stood there. "He's taken a turn for the worse. That Dark boy you hit. He's in a coma."

"What?"

"Whether or not he'll make it, that's in doubt."

Frederick felt the need to dress. He sat there pulling on his jeans.

"Where are you going?"

"Out to the hospital."

"Oh, no. No. I doubt they'll let you in—to see him."

"Coma. Got to."

"We'll have to meet with Mr. Bulge first opportunity tomorrow."

"What good will that do?"

"We'll see. Night now. A coma. That's not the end of the world, is it? People go into comas all the time. They come out of comas. You've got to see what's next. Mr. Bulge will tell us what's next."

He lay there for a half hour, contemplating it all, and then he dressed, then went down the stairs in his sock feet, carrying his shoes. He got those on, then got in that second car and took off. Now he wasn't drunk and besides there wasn't much traffic. He sped, doing fifty in a thirty-five zone, then fifty-five. Pissed. He was pissed. He felt like taking risks. He took one when he saw the yellow light way ahead and decided he could surely shoot straight through that, but he couldn't, and he wasn't even to the intersection when it turned red. But no cars coming, and no cop cars in sight. He slowed a bit.

In ten more minutes he was in the parking lot of the hospital.

Snow was falling.

He made it through a waiting room with several TV monitors with world news. There was a school shooting somewhere. Where, he didn't catch. He made it to the patient information desk. A woman he didn't recognize gave him an expectant look, and then said "May I help you?"

"Horatio Dark. I want to see Horatio Dark."

She turned to her computer screen. She took a moment. "It's Room 303, but I'm sorry, no visitors—except family members."

"Can you tell me why?"

"Because that's hospital policy."

And then it sprang to his lips. "But I'm his brother."

She smiled. She looked again at the computer. "I'm sorry, but he has no brother."

He nodded again. "Are they up there? With him? His family?"

"I can't tell you that."

"Oh." And then he said, "I understand."

"Good," she said.

He took off for the elevator. In a minute or two, he was approaching Room 303. The door was open, about halfway.

At first he stood a few feet away from that doorway. And then he moved forward, step by step. He peeked in. A woman was looking down at Horatio Dark lying there. She was fondling his hair. She was smiling, or half smiling, and humming something to herself. And then she began singing a tune of some sort. It sounded like a lullaby. And then she looked up and spotted him.

"Yes? Did you want something?"

"I got the wrong room."

She glared at him. "No, you didn't. You got the right room. You're that bad boy, aren't you? That one."

He looked at her, then looked quickly away at some sort of machine with green lights blinking. Then he looked back. "Which boy?"

"Don't play games with me. I've talked to the police, young man. I know who you are and I saw your face in the yearbook. A big smile. You're not smiling now, are you? You feeling guilty? Is that it? For killing my poor little boy?"

"Killing?" he said.

"I'd think you would. Look at my poor son, lying like this. Dead to the world. Just dead. Dead."

"Dead?"

"He might as well be."

She might be about to cry, but she just gently stroked Horatio Dark's hair. And then she seemed to become absorbed by something, some thought, something. He watched her for a few long minutes. Had she fainted?

"I'm sorry. I didn't mean to. It just sort of... happened."

"Sure," came her voice. "Sure."

He started to leave.

"Come here. Step this way."

"What? What do you—"

"I need help moving him."

He stood there. Then he shook his head. "I'd better not do that. You'd better get a nurse, hadn't you? Hadn't you better get a nurse—some male nurse—a big one—for something like that?"

She laughed, a cackle. "You can beat him half to death, but you can't be bothered to help move him so he's more comfortable in bed?"

"I didn't... beat him half to death. I threw just one punch after—"

"I've heard your flimsy excuse of a story. I don't want to hear it again. Get over here."

"Huh? But—"

"You're just full of buts, aren't you? I suppose I'll have to move him. A lady my size isn't exactly supposed to do such a thing with a big son like mine. He was the hardest of the three to bring through the birth canal—did you know that? Hmm?"

"No."

"Well, he was. I paid dearly for that. I certainly did. I knew he was going to be big, but my god, that big? And yet the likes of you—how tall are you, anyway?"

"Five-seven... or so."

"Don't know? Well, I'd say five-seven. And you toppled this young man here, just an inch shy of six feet, and nearly killed him. Maybe you have killed him. Did you use brass knuckles or something? He's in a coma. Isn't that the first stage toward death? I could just die myself knowing that. I could. I have already."

"Maybe... maybe his doctor... maybe he'll know."

"You assume it's a he—I notice things like that."

"Oh. Who is it?"

"Some Arab or Indian or someone like that. They know things we don't, so that's good. That's real good."

She popped something from her purse and chewed.

"I've got to go," he said.

"Sure you do. Just go. Go away. If he dies, he dies. We've got to accept things like that, don't we? I believe that. We're fated. Do you? Do you believe that?"

"I don't know. I hope not."

"Go now."

"Yes, ma'am."

"Don't you dare call me *ma'am*."

"Oh, no—no, I won't."

"And I don't ever want to see you again—unless it's be-hind bars."

"I don't... want that," he said.

"I'll just bet you don't."

2

Horatio Dark had called his girlfriend a "bitch." Only that wasn't exactly the truth because she wasn't exactly his girlfriend. He wanted her to be his girlfriend; he'd lusted after her for a whole year, but she barely took notice of him. Still, there were a few moments at her locker, and a few at his locker, and a few in the Geography classroom, and a few more down in the lunchroom, a few in study hall, and once or twice outside, when she'd smiled at him. A sort of vagrant smiling, a smile in passing. And he'd smiled back, perhaps too heartily. How lovely her smile. How sensual her body. Those lips. That hair. Silky.

And there, at that party, Horatio Dark had stood by, lounging against the wall with a drink of whiskey and had said casually. "Lilac? What the hell kind of name is that? I had to laugh the first time I heard it. But in bed, what a tigress. Huh?"

"What?" said Frederick. "What did you say?"

"In bed. You need that repeated, do you?"

"You bastard," said Frederick.

"She's a bitch," said Dark, smirking. "A cute little bitch. But a bitch all the same."

And that's when he'd hauled off and let him have it,

right on the chin.

He thought he heard bones snapping.

And that's when, a second later, the man toppled over. In that regard, though, Frederick was lucky because a few guys standing next to Dark caught the bastard before he landed on his head.

"Help him up," yelled one of them.

"I'm calling 911," said Frederick.

And he did.

*　*　*

Surely that bit got out and Lilac Johnson knew all about it. How Dark had said what she'd done, how he'd called her what he'd called her, and how Frederick had come to her defense. Which, if one thought much about it, made him look damned presumptuous. What right had he to come to her defense? She wasn't his girlfriend, and here he was acting like she was. Still, maybe she liked it. She ought to.

The funny thing, not haha funny, but just odd, was that he hadn't intended to shoot his fist out at all. It was like his brain said do it, and he'd not had an ounce of control over it.

He toyed with his cell phone. He had her cell phone number, not that she'd given it to him in a romantic way; he and she, a few years back, were teamed up with a few others on a class project in History, and they'd all exchanged numbers. He still had hers, of course. He fiddled with his phone for about an hour, and then he punched in the numbers.

He waited.

*　*　*

The two of them stood outside of her house. It was a two-story white house, an old one, a Victorian one. They stood on the sidewalk, and now and then he stuck his foot on the curb.

"I heard," she said. "I'm cold."

He wanted to put his arm around her. What he wouldn't give to put his arm around her.

Her eyes flashed at him. "Why'd you do it, anyway?"

"I wanted to."

"Uh huh, and why is that?"

"Because." But he couldn't say it.

"Well, you needn't have. I just came out here to tell you in case you're spreading it around that I wanted you to. I didn't, and I don't."

"He called you a bad name."

"So?"

He started to touch her arm covered up by a blue wool coat. "I didn't want—"

"I don't care. I don't care what you did or didn't want. I'm not your girl—okay?"

"Okay," he said. But it wasn't.

Silence. And then: "What'll you get for that? Jail time?"

"I don't know."

She started in. "Well, the next time, check. Okay?"

"Sure."

She turned around. "You going to stand there like that?"

"No." He turned to go to his car, that second car, which looked unsightly with a big dent in the fender, parked alongside the curb, piled high with snow. His front bumper was mashed against a pile of it, but where else was there to park? He wasn't parking in her driveway.

"Go! Will you?" she snapped.

In a few days he'd no longer be living with his father. He'd found a second-floor apartment with an outside entrance. The old lady who rented it made him put down a deposit of one hundred and seventy-five with the first month's rent due as soon as he moved in. He had six hundred still in his account from some odd jobs he'd picked up, including janitorial work on weekends at the school, and summers, and that would pretty much clean him out.

That apartment. He could bring in girls with that outside entrance. It was to the back of the house, and you had to walk up a flight of rickety wooden steps, but it was safe. The thing was, there was to be no member of the opposite sex allowed. "I run a respectable house," the old woman had said. "And I do hear. If I hear a young lady up there laughing or carrying on, that'll be that."

"Sure," he'd said.

"Sure, what?"

"No girls."

"Or women. One young man had a whore up there. A prostitute. Can you imagine that? The noise they made. How disgusting."

"Oh."

"It's in the lease. You haven't seen that yet, but it's in there. And no late rent. Don't drink up your money and then expect me to take up the slack. I won't do it. That's in the lease."

"I understand."

"One hundred and seventy-five per month. That's a steal."

"Good. I'll take it."

"First month's rent of one seventy-five is due as soon as you move in. And that's fair. Better than you'll find lots of places."

"Okay," he said.

She ran a hand through her white hair. "Are you a good boy?"

"Huh?"

"I asked whether you're a good boy."

"Sure."

"I hope so. I wouldn't take you into my house if I didn't think you were. This isn't like an apartment group, you know. You'd be living in my house. Right above where I sleep. And where I spend a lot of my time on various things. I'm a great reader! Are you? I can hear practically any goings-on up there." She pointed up at her ceiling. A rotary fan was up there. But being winter, it was dead still.

"I'll be okay." Except, he thought, for that bit about girls. And women. That was his very purpose of getting this little haunt in the first place. If he wanted a room, he had one back at his father's house. Of course the old lady knew it.

"You're in high school," she said.

"Yes."

She shook her head. "What do you learn there? Anything? Anything at all?" She expected an answer. "Well," he said.

"You'd best behave. No drinking! No parties!"

"No."

"And don't think I can't hear tabs of beer cans popping. I sure can."

"Beer cans," he said.

"But you're not old enough to drink. And so you'd better not."

"No, no," he said.

"Now, then, I've got to call it a night."

It was nine o'clock. Was she actually intending on going to bed?

"All right," he said. And then they parted.

Well, it was better than nothing. It was the cheapest

place he could get. Just be quiet, he thought. And make sure the bed springs don't sing too loud.

*　*　*

He went back to that bar. He had two beers, then a whiskey. He thought about a lot of things. He wasn't eighteen yet and he had his own apartment. He wouldn't, of course, say anything about that apartment to the school. The principal, that is. He needn't know. And in line with that, he wouldn't spread the word. He'd keep it to himself.

It was growing eleven o'clock, and he had a History paper to write. He might not get it done. He might have to make up an excuse. He kept getting this image of Lilac in his head. How pretty she was. How late it was, but how pretty she looked in the snow. It occurred to him that she acted the way she did because she was just embarrassed and actually wanted him to approach her and take her in his arms. He'd been a fool not to. He imagined the two of them in that apartment of his. He imagined a bottle of wine. He imagined a lot more.

He had his cell phone before him. What if he called? It wasn't that late. What if he told her exactly what he felt, what he'd been feeling for months now, almost a whole year. What if he talked it up and didn't back down? What if she didn't end the call?

He was on his fourth beer when he punched in those numbers.

When there was no answer, he left the bar and headed to his father's second-hand junker. He was dizzy. He was seeing double. But he had to go where he had to go. Because let's face it, he told himself, he had done this deed for her. He hadn't hesitated. His fist had shot out and knocked Horatio Dark over—because why? Because he deserved it. And him, he deserved some recognition and appreciation for what he'd done. Damn right he did.

Here he was maybe a murderer, and this is all he got?—this woman, or girl, he had stood up for sloughed him off like that? It wasn't right, and now and then you had to declare what was right and what wasn't.

3

Take what's yours. That's what a guy at a New Year's Eve party told him, on an icy night when he'd had way too much to drink and was falling down, and then went off to vomit in the men's restroom. And then he came back out and said to this guy, a college senior: "You mean it? You mean actually do that?"

"Why would I say it if I didn't mean it?"

"Right," said Frederick.

"Take it or leave it. It's up to you."

The guy had a vicious, bulldog sort of face, with big teeth. He reminded Frederick of some boxer he'd seen on TV, also with big teeth. He was afraid to disagree. Only why disagree? He liked the idea.

"I'm going for that," he said. He never caught the guy's name, and he hadn't asked.

"Up to you."

He came up with a name: Brutal. This guy's name was *Brutal*.

"You're mine," he said, standing out on the sidewalk,

almost precisely where he'd stood before, only then with her, now by himself.

He saw some sort of movement, a flutter of red curtains against the light.

Awake. She was awake. That was her room up there. It was hers all right. He knew that because once, during their team project, he'd ridden in a car with her, squeezed right next to her, and once she'd gotten out and headed for her front door, the driver had waited until her light came on. That was a sign, she said, that all was okay. And the teacher-driver said how you couldn't be sure these days, could you? You never knew. You just never knew.

He watched for signs of movement. What if he caught her undressing?

It had started to rain ice pellets. He wanted to be inside—with her—up in that room. Only he wished it was dark. That was how he wished it would be, him and her, in the dark. Going for each other's bodies. A steamy thing. Cold outside, but warm under those covers.

He went for his cell phone in his jeans. Pulled it out. He didn't hesitate, not this time. He keyed her number in. He waited, watching the cranberry-colored curtains.

"Yes," came a voice, her voice. He knew that voice. Distinctly female. "What are you calling me for?"

"I know it's late. But I was needing to speak. Just to speak."

"Yeah? About what?"

"Us."

"Us—what?"

"You and me."

"Are you sick or something?"

"No. I'm not. Just let me come up there, and I'll show you."

He immediately regretted what he'd just said.

"Ha! Now why would I do that?"

"Because."

"Ha! That's what they say girls, or women, say. Are you a girl or a woman?"

"No. Just let me up there." He was heading now toward the red front door.

"I'm calling the cops. So unless you want to be hauled in for that, plus the other, just stick around."

"Please!" he yelled. "I need to see you. I've got something to say, and I can't say it over the phone."

"Oh, sure."

"Please!"

He was begging, and he didn't like begging. "One thing you don't want to do," said Brutal, "is plead and beg. You got it?"

But he must have her. She must not deny him what he needed, wanted, desired with every ounce of his being.

"I'm coming down," she said. "For one minute. But that's it."

"Okay," he said. "Good."

He tried to think. He tried not to think. It had to be spontaneous. He would know what to say when the time came.

Suddenly the door opened, and she was hurrying by him and making her way down the sidewalk to the edge of the yard. He followed.

She faced him. "What do you want?"

"You."

"What?"

"I want you."

She gave him a shove. "Oh, you do, do you?"

"Yes."

"Well, I don't want you. I've got a boyfriend already, and even if I didn't, you can bet I could do better than you. I'd go into a convent first!" She shoved him again, but this time harder.

"Let me come upstairs with you," he said. "You'll see."

"What? What am I going to see?"

"A place. A place I'm going to have. In a few days, I'm going to have it. I just need you to have it with me."

"You little worm."

"I could make you happy," he said. "Who's that boyfriend of yours?"

"No one you know. He's from out of town."

"What's so good about him?"

She shook her head. "I'm leaving now."

He went for her coat. She shoved him again. He bounced against the tree.

"Listen," he said. "I've got a car coming too. A sports car. Red. You'd like it."

"I'm sure."

"No, I do."

"Where is it?"

"I'll have it soon, just not yet."

She was on her way to the front door, stomping through the snow, the ice pellets coming down harder. Her coat was shiny with them.

He rushed toward her. "I can have it tomorrow! And there's a place out of town, a good drinking place—"

"Not interested," she said, and the door slammed.

He spent the night on the internet looking for red sports cars. And then he found a page with a bright, shiny red one, and he shot it to her. He wrote a note: *This is going to be my baby in one week. Just one week. No, make that a day or two!*

No answer. He checked his email several times an hour, but no answer.

❦ ❦ ❦

"Here's the thing," said Brutal at that New Year's Eve party. "Here's the thing. You tell yourself you're going to do it, and you do it. See? Get me? You don't hesitate. You don't let some little obstacle—you might think it's big, but it's not—you don't let that get in your way. You do whatever. You follow?"

That's when he left. That guy Brutal was nuts.

Why'd he go out to her place? Why? Why?

❧ ❧ ❧

He went to classes. He tried to prepare for that court appearance. His lawyer walked him through it. He knew all about this kind of thing, he said, and so just listen. Do this. Do that. Answer this. Answer that. Act like you're a good guy, a respectable citizen. Wear a suit, a dark one. If you don't own one, go buy one. And not some cheap suit, either, a respectable looking one that fits right. Don't get a tan suit. Dark. White shirt, blue or brown tie. You've been accused of something, but you're innocent as the day is long. Comprehend?

"He's in a coma. How is that innocent?"

"He'll come out of it. And he'll be a better man for it."

"How is that?"

"Didn't he insult your girlfriend? He had it coming."

"You want me to say that?"

"No, no! No, don't say that. No! Don't say anything close to that. Just set the judge up to say it. Set the jury up to say it. Don't you, no matter what you say, say that. You want to go to jail, you say that."

"No. No, I don't want to."

"Okay, then."

He went to school. He flunked a test or two. He moved stuff into his apartment, paid the first month's rent. Where was the second coming from? Oh, well.

He lay around in his bed imagining Lilac up there with him. In that very bed with him. Under the covers, the lights off. Married to her. Sort of married.

He told himself what he really wanted out of life. He wanted:

1. To go free and not go to jail. And not to pay a fine. Because how could he pay it?
2. Have Lilac all to himself.
3. Not have Horatio Dark die.

He supposed #3 ought to be #1. No, both #1 and #3 were of equal weight. No, you bastard, #3 was the most important—sure it was. Still, how could he say that #1 wasn't a big ticket item? Sure it was. And... #2 was of enormous importance, or he wouldn't even be concerned with #1 or #3.

Damn, he thought. Damn.

❧ ❧ ❧

It was snowing again, and it was late. Real late. It was past three in the morning, actually, but he was feeling a need, a great need.

He could feel it pulsing in him. It was like something pressing against the back of his head. It demanded he do something.

Five beers. He'd lost count, but it had to be five—at least five. The bartender was looking at him with an air about him. Those black eyes that hovered over dark-rimmed frames. The guy was old, real old. Fifty, sixty.

Well, it was time to leave anyway.

He headed out into the night.

He wished he had that red car and could arrive at her house in style. He wished he could make an appearance, park it under that tree along the curb, get out, head right to her front door, and there she would be: waiting for him, in a skimpy nightie.

Now that he'd moved, he had no car at all. "You're on

your own now," said his father. "Besides, what if my good car goes out?" So he was on foot, and it was a mile and a half at least.

He made it through the downtown, past the stores, past some late-night pizza joints, past a donut shop, past a night spot, loud with jazz. He was soon back in the neighborhoods, and then, feet half frozen, hands stuffed in his parka pockets, he arrived.

Straight to the front door he went.

That red front door.

He knocked. Once, just once. A light knock.

He felt dizzy. That beer.

No sounds. He could hear only the tinkling of ice in the trees.

He knocked again.

He thought he heard something. It was a scratching sound. Was it a cat?

He knocked again, then again, then again.

A voice rang out. "Who is it?"

"It's me. Frederick Weber."

The door remained closed.

"Just a minute."

The door opened. "What are you doing here? My daughter said something about you. What do you want?"

"To see your daughter."

He was inside now, a few feet, and the man moved aside and shut the door.

"About what? Say, you smell. You've been drinking, haven't you?"

"Beer."

"You follow me. We'll get you some coffee and see what's going on here."

Her father hurried into the kitchen. He followed.

"I want to see Lilac," he said.

"Oh, you do? What for?"

"Because."

"That's no answer."

"I want to tell her something."

"Private, huh." He was putting on the coffee. "You realize what time it is? Do you always go around drunk at a time like this—what is it? Four o'clock? And bother people when they're trying to sleep?"

"No. It's the first time I've done it."

"And why is that?"

"I'm in love with your daughter. That's why."

"Um! Is that right? Well, what she's said about you tells me you're not in the running at all, son. Besides, she's got a boyfriend already."

He stood at the coffee pot, his back to Frederick.

"That won't last long," said Frederick.

"Huh? How is that?"

"Because I told you. I'm in love with her."

"That's too bad."

"No, it's not."

"Calm down." He grabbed a cup. "This is reheated coffee, but it's still good. We'll get you sobered up; then you can walk back where you came from. In precisely an hour. Or I'll take you. I'd probably better take you."

Suddenly in the doorway stood Lilac, in a robe. "What in hell?" she said.

"I'm getting him sobered up," said her father.

"Get that red car yet?" she said.

"No. But I will."

She leaned in the doorway. "I'll just bet."

"I will."

"What car?" said her father.

"A red sports car," said Frederick. "I sent her a picture."

"Anybody can send a picture."

"I'll get it."

"And then what?" she said.

"And then I'll take you for a ride."

"That's laughable."

That stung. "Why is it? Why is that laughable?"

Her father pointed at his coffee cup. "Sip that. He's drunk," he said.

"He's always drunk. He was drunk when he hit that Dork boy."

"What? Which boy?"

"Horatio. That one."

"Oh, my! That boy is very dangerous. Not a good boy, from what I've heard."

"How is that?" said Frederick.

"He's setting himself up for a life of crime. Of course he's got relatives in the mob, so why wouldn't he?"

"Mob?"

"That's right." Lilac nodded.

"No," said Frederick.

"Yes. He's going to court over it."

"They'll let you go. Who's the judge?"

"Barnhart."

"Hard to say. Tough on crime."

"I'm going to bed," said Lilac. She gave him a look—was it exasperation? —and then she was gone.

He drank coffee for an hour, and then he left. He was back at his apartment in another hour, and thinking everything over.

Her father got a little weird over that coffee. He began to spike it with a pint. "She might be pregnant," he said. "That's not you, is it?"

"No, sir. I can't even—"

"What?"

"Get near her."

"Well, it takes that," said her father.

He wanted to get near her—that's for sure. He listened for noises below. There wasn't much. This and that thing moving was all. A cough or two.

4

The next afternoon, after classes let out, Frederick made his way to his lawyer's office. Mr. Bulge waved him in. He was on the phone.

He nodded a lot. He said "Um, huh" a lot. Then he put the phone down and said, "Come with me. Got a party to attend—birthday party. Good looking woman, too, so I'll bet you'll like that. Come with me."

He seemed different.

Bulge hurried him out to the parking lot.

"I just wanted to know—"

"Got to hurry. Late for the party."

He flicked his remote, and he motioned for Frederick to get in the Lexus. Mr. Bulge got in the driver's seat. Before Frederick was buckled up, he backed up fast, stopped, the brakes screeching, and then he shot down the lot filled with cars.

"Birthday party?"

"Beautiful young woman. I'll bet you'd strike a man if he said anything bad about that lovely little number."

"How old?"

"Um. Twenty-five, I think. No, twenty-four. No, twenty-six. Young, though. Older than you, of course. You're what?"

"Eighteen."

"Why aren't you twenty-one? Don't you know that's a man's prime age? Everything after that's downhill."

"I'm just not. I will be, though."

"Do you believe in hedonism?"

"What?"

"What's this thing you want to know?" He shot down the street and honked a car from pulling out—on Frederick's side.

"This Horatio Dark. Is his family in the mob—a crime family?"

"Sure is. Well, let me amend that. Could be. Hard to say."

"You don't know?"

"Lots of things a lawyer doesn't know. We'll just have to wait and see."

"Whether he's in the mob? Or, I mean, his family?"

"No, not his family—him, if anyone's in the mob. Family could be, sure. You never know. You know, you should know your opponent and know him well. You've got to plan, see. If he's in the mob, that's important to know, isn't it?" He was lighting a cigarette, no hands on the steering wheel.

"Uh, please," said Frederick. "Please. Don't have a wreck."

"Wreck. I've driven for over thirty years. You think I'm about to have a wreck? You mind if I smoke?"

"No—well, yes. Second-hand smoke, you know."

The window came down. Bulge flicked the cigarette out the window. "Look, you've got to prepare. Have you been preparing—at all?"

They were now getting on the interstate. A complex of high-rise office buildings rose to his right a half mile or more off the interstate. Steel and glass. A black cloud etched the blue sky.

"No—I don't know what to do."

"Well, look into that young man being a mobster. What's he doing right now? You been tracking him?"

"He's in a coma."

"Oh, that's right. That's right. She's certainly a beauty. You'll be pleased. You like cake?"

"Yes."

"Ice cream?"

"Of course."

"I can't promise anything. That's the way it is in the legal profession. You can't promise a thing. Not a single thing."

He was worrying at his tie, adjusting it. He was lighting another cigarette.

"Are you thinking of something—something I should know about?"

"You don't know?"

"No."

"Well, it's not important. I'm sure it's not important to a young man like you with your whole life before you. Not at all important."

"What's not?"

"A thing like this. Like this birthday party. Not being invited. And after all I've done for that little beauty. Well, she's not a little beauty. She's a big one. I don't mean heavy or anything—oh no, not at all. What I mean is important. And no, I wasn't invited."

"But you're going?"

"Yes, I am because it's only right. I could piss and moan, but it's better to just show up and let things, you know, take their course."

"Do you think he is in the mob?" asked Frederick, "a guy his age? I thought mobsters were older, generally speaking."

"Oh, no, no. They recruit them young. He could be a foot soldier. Now, if he is I'd watch my windows. But then that's only an expression. I'd curtain them. I wouldn't be seen. I'd go into hiding."

"But is he in the mob? What do you know? Do you know anything at all?"

"Just tales, that's it. Probably an enforcer. Kicking in ribs, breaking fingers, breaking jaws. That's the way a lot of them start out."

They were pulling into a large office complex, at least thirty stories high. "Well, I... I don't know—"

"Well, now, we're here. You haven't been under specific threats, have you?"

"No."

"Oh, shoot. Then why worry? You'd be dead by now, given their track record. Unless you've gone into hiding. Have you?"

"No." Except he was about to mention that apartment he'd rented.

"He's an enforcer or he isn't. As simple as that."

❧ ❧ ❧

"Look at that," said Mr. Bulge. "Isn't she a beauty? Have you ever seen such, such—"

"Um," said Frederick. She was indeed a beauty. Blond, sensual, arousing. He tried to think of different words. "Who is she—I mean to you?"

"Secretary. Was, anyway. Come." He pulled Frederick along.

They were heading straight for her.

"Hello, Missy," said Bulge.

"Hello, Mr. Bulge."

"Oh, no, dear. Edmund."

She smiled.

"Happy birthday, dear."

A number of small groups had gathered in the large

room, with a vaulted ceiling.

"Thank you, sir."

He put out his hand and touched her arm. "I've missed you."

"Now, now. I went on. To another firm. That's frequent, isn't it? Isn't it now, Mr. Bulge."

"I suppose it is." He rubbed his bearded chin.

She was still smiling. "How is everything. Is this a new intern?"

"Oh, no, sorry, sorry," Bulge grabbed him by the shoulder. "This is Frederick Weber. A client of mine."

"Indeed. Civil or criminal?"

"Now, now," said Bulge. "You're too inquisitive, sweetie." He laid a hand on hers. "Aren't you now?"

"I might be." She was looking directly at Frederick, and he was drowning in those blue eyes. Her chin, so shapely, her cheeks so...

"Now, now," said Bulge. "You oughtn't be. You're not in my employ anymore."

"You won't let me forget that, will you, Mr. Bulge."

"Edmund, dearest."

"Oh gosh."

"You know," said Bulge, "I was telling my intern here, Frederick, all about you."

"Intern? I thought you said..."

"Well, yes, but let's just say he is an intern. He could be, couldn't he?"

Her eyes were dancing over him, so blue, so sparkly. "I guess so. Sure, though he's kind of young... aren't you, Frederick?"

"Not so young. Not all that young."

"And why do you say that?" That smile, and those eyes swallowing him whole.

"Well, I've got my own apartment. With an outside entrance."

"Oh, bully!" She took his hand. "Is that an invitation?"

"No, no," Bulge jumped in. "No, no, of course not. He's in enough trouble as it is, isn't that right, Fred?"

"Frederick."

"Sure."

"Trouble?" said the beauty. "A lot or a little?"

"Not so much," said Frederick.

"Come," she said, and took his hand. She led him away from Mr. Bulge, who, as Frederick noticed as they walked off, was rubbing his beard with a grim look on those fat lips.

"What?"

"Now, then. You want me, don't you?"

"Uh, yes. Yes."

"Well, then, you can have me—if you pay the requisite price. I'll bet Mr. Bulge there never mentioned what I really do for a living, did he?"

"No."

"And you've got an apartment. How sweet. How old are you?"

"Eighteen."

"Why aren't you older? But go ahead, show me an ID, if you don't mind."

He took out his billfold, looked in Mr. Bulge's direction, and then removed his driver's license. He slipped it into her waiting palm.

"Um huh," she said and returned it.

"You see," he said.

"Oh, I see. But you're not quite eighteen, are you?"

"Almost."

"Well, almost isn't good enough. Come to me when you're eighteen. Okay, sweetie?"

"Okay."

"Do you have the money it takes?"

"Huh? How much?"

She laughed. "More than you've got I'll just bet."

"Tell me. Do tell me anyway."

She stared at him. Then an incipient smile. "You want to know, don't you? You just have to know."

"Yes, please."

"Five hundred an hour. Go five hours and you get a twenty-percent discount on the next five." She gave him a grin. It was a sly one.

"Oh, damn. No... I don't have that kind of money. No."

"Well, for the kind of pleasure you'd be getting from me, you'd just have to have that kind of money. Get it and we'll talk. She came forth with a card and slipped it in his palm. "It hurts not to have what you want. Don't delay too long." And then she returned to Bulge.

✻ ✻ ✻

"Is he a mobster or not, that's our question, isn't it?" said Bulge speeding them through traffic.

"You think he is?"

"I doubt it."

"But I thought you said—"

"He could be. He certainly could be. Isn't she a pretty one?"

"Yes. Yes, she is." His inwards were crashing down thinking of her. Those lips, those eyes, that soft neck. Those soft hands. Those lovely arms. Those sweet ears.

"I'm not saying he's a mobster, don't get me wrong, and don't say it in court, but we'll get our research done, and we'll certainly find out if he is. I'm thinking maybe he is."

"Then why didn't he knock me flat?"

Mr. Bulge laughed. "Oh, they're as vulnerable as anyone on this earth. You hit him just right. Nailed him. That'll come out in court, of course. It'll look like you knew exactly what you were doing."

"But I didn't. I just struck out."

"Over that girl, your girlfriend."

"Well, she's not exactly—"

"And so what were you and Missy having your little whispering session over?"

"Uh. Well, nothing really."

"Well, that's her all right. She's a lot of nothing. Beautiful to look at but... not really approachable. Not when it comes down to it. If you read me."

"Sure. I do."

"How's that?"

"How's what?"

"You reading me."

"I do."

"Uh, huh. When we get there, you make your way back to that apartment of yours, but get back here at five tomorrow, and we'll talk."

"Okay."

"You think you're something, don't you?"

"Huh?"

"Everything in this world comes with a price tag. You keep that in mind."

"I will."

"Good for you."

He dropped Frederick off in front of his building, and Frederick hoofed it on home, or rather to his apartment.

5

A knocking on his door. He got up off his bed where he'd been napping and went straight to it. He could see her through the window in the door, once he'd yanked the shade.

He opened it.

"Yes?"

"Young man. What was that about going out in the pitch-dark down those stairs? I can hear practically everything you do up here. Every foot on every step. And I don't like my sleep disturbed. I thought I made that clear."

"I'm sorry. I had a necessary trip."

"Oh? For what? What was so necessary?"

"What?"

"That's what I asked."

"My father was ill."

"Oh. Is that right?" She sized him up with gray eyes, practically the same color as her hair, tied up in a bun.

"He's doing okay—now."

"Just keep in mind that I don't like noise. The world is full of it. My little house is my escape from such noise, such terrible noise. Do you understand?"

"Yes, ma'am. I do."

"So… if you run a vacuum cleaner or play music, or do whatever young men your age do—whatever loud, noisy things you come up with—then be sure it's before eight at night. Nothing after eight. Am I getting through?"

"Yes, ma'am."

"Good. The same with the TV."

"I don't have a TV."

She looked around. "So you don't. You don't have much of anything. Have you moved in—completely?"

"Not completely."

"Goodness."

And then she was gone.

❧ ❧ ❧

He shelled out all the money he had on his bed. He counted it. Four hundred dollars—or so.

His cell phone rang.

Lilac.

He answered. "Yes? It's you," he said.

"No. It's not. It's her father," said the voice.

"Oh."

"Did you make it back all right? Hoofing it at such a weary hour?"

"Yes."

"It was not smart what you did, but I forgive, and Lilac forgives. Now, the thing to do is to reason together. What are we after here? What are our goals?"

"Goals? I have only one goal," said Frederick. "And that is your daughter."

"I've decided to write the judge a letter," said Lilac's father. "And what I say, son, will carry some weight."

His gut tightened. "What will you say?"

"I'm not pleased with your behavior. I'm not pleased at

all. Coming over here at all hours of the night. Thinking you can take my daughter off to bed with you. She has no intention of going up to bed with you. You mistake her intention of being in a nightie if you think that."

He started to say, "But she wasn't in a nightie—she was in a robe," but he caught himself. He guessed he wasn't supposed to notice that sort of thing. "I had no such intention."

"Oh, of course you did. And do. My daughter is not for sale, son. That's the point I want to make. She's saving it all for that special bond called marriage. That doesn't mean much these days, but to me it means a lot. To hold that little grand-baby in my hands, to know it was not the product of an illicit union, such as my daughter herself was—well, that would make me very proud. Are you interested in such a union, son?"

"Yes. Yes, I am."

"How soon? How soon, son?"

My god. "Uh, as soon as I can." He thought of dearest, slim, curvy Lilac Johnson in her nightie with cleavage. He thought of the light in her room going off. He thought of —

"How about Friday next week? This coming Friday?"

"What? Why so—"

"Fast? You can't know really, can you? Do you have that red car yet? That sports car?"

"No. No, but I'm going to get it soon. That's for sure. I'm going to get work, you know, even with my classes and all, and I'll buy it. You bet."

"Sure. Look, Friday, I can get the two of you with our minister."

Bona fide, he thought. The real thing. A real wife. "Friday?" That was the date of his court appearance—if it was still on for that date. Bulge said he couldn't be sure.

He mentioned it to Lilac's father.

"Oh, don't worry about the judge. Knowing what you're

doing here, he'll let you off. Unless the boy dies in that coma, but then... given his being of a very questionable ilk, well, I think the judge will get with the jury prior to the date and ask that his feelings toward this thing be... you know, taken into strong consideration."

"He could do that?"

"Judge Barnhart can do whatever he wants, son."

"But why the... why the rush?"

Silence. Then, "What do you think about having a child, son. A little boy?"

That soon? This soon? "I don't know. I mean I'd first like to... you know—"

"Play around? Oh, there'll be plenty of time for that. She's hardly showing."

"What?"

"That boyfriend she might have told you about? Well, sir, he won't go the route, but I'm hoping you will. A little boy all your own—and hers too."

"How do you know?"

"Oh, we don't. Not yet. But if it is, it'll probably be a great athlete like his father. Shoulders wide, legs strong, stomach tight—a six pack, you know—hair neat and combed. Just visualize him on that field. Hers, yours— and his, of course. I can see it all, can't you? I can visualize it. There, there—do you? Do you see it? Ah!"

He said nothing.

"Can't you?"

"Have you... have you been drinking, sir?"

"Oh, no—not that much. No."

"Where's Lilac? Can I speak to Lilac? Can I speak to her?"

Silence. "Um."

"I can't?"

"Um."

"I want to."

"She's asleep. I think."

"Does she know about this—this plan of yours?"

"And yours?"

"Well, as long as I..."

"Well. Look, that car. She's taken with that car. I suggest you show up in that car next time, and that'll make all the difference in the world."

"Really, but—"

He kept talking but no one was on the line. He called back, but no answer.

❧ ❧ ❧

The next afternoon, he was at the dealer, and he was looking in the showroom, and there it was. Sleek, what lines, what curvatures, and red—as red as could be. Blood red. Such stylish curves. How full but trim!

"Would you like to take this out for a little spin, sir?" asked a man in a white shirt with a large blue bowtie.

"I would."

"There's one out on the lot in the back. "Let's get you a key, and let's get you on the road with that little baby."

"Yes, sir."

The man disappeared into his office and then came forward jingling a set of keys. He handed them to Frederick. "Just follow me."

He did, and they arrived at a red car, identical to the one in the showroom. It felt like it wanted to go. To go, go. It felt as though it were taking a deep breath. This, he thought, is the essence of pleasure. The very heart of it. *There are other paths,* he recalled reading. *Pleasure is overrated.*

No, he thought. No, it's not.

"Now, then, you're an experienced driver, I assume."

"Oh, yes, sir."

"Well, good. All right," and he leaned over and inserted

the key into the ignition. "Then take it for a spin and be back here soon. It's an expensive car. Where do you work, just out of curiosity?"

He waited, debated. "At a law office."

"Oh, which one?"

"Does it matter?" said Frederick. "After all, they're all so alike. If you catch my drift."

"Oh, I do, sir. Yes, of course."

And Frederick got in the seat of the red car and was on the road in a matter of a minute or less.

❦ ❦ ❦

It took but ten minutes to arrive at her house. He didn't sit in the red car and wait. He didn't sit there and wonder. He didn't sit there and puzzle over his options. He got out of the car and hurried straight for the front door—and knocked.

He knocked but once, and there she stood.

"What did he tell you?" she said, and gave him a look that hurt his eyes.

"Oh, well, that—"

"He told you I'm pregnant? He told you that?"

"Yes. Sort of."

"Sort of? Come in. Don't just stand there. Oh," and with him halfway in, she said, "the car! You got the car! Oh, it is so beautiful. So... heavenly. Oh, my, my, my! May I see it? May I ride in it?"

"Sure. Of course. Sure."

She took his hand. They hurried to the car. He had the keys in his pocket. He hurried around to the driver's side. She was in already.

They took off. At first he drove slowly, watching every little thing, but then he kept watching the speedometer. Get it up, get it up. One hundred and forty... was it possible? Was it? He got it going, going, going as they took the on-ramp onto the interstate, and he was soon passing semis and weaving in and out of traffic. He was shooting by everything, buildings, suburban areas, noise barrier walls, into the snow-covered countryside, over the river on the long, long bridge. Where were they going? He had no idea. His foot just told him to keep going. And fast.

"It's his," she said. "It's his, but he won't claim it."

"Huh?"

"I said, it's his, but he won't own up to it."

"He won't, will he? Well, I will."

"What?"

"That's me," he said. "I'll claim anything. You bet."

His knee was punched. He yelped.

"That's how you think of it? Like something you put on the layaway plan. Something that... that ordinary."

He turned and laid a hand on her knee. "No, no. No. It's his, but it'll be mine—too. Ours, I mean. All the way." And, then, still looking at her, at those sweet red lips, that cute little nose, he said, "If you'll just have me."

"I might just put it up for adoption," she said. "But better yet, an abortion. Yes, that. I just might."

He had his eyes on the road. He knew of a place up ahead—off on a blacktop maybe a mile off the interstate. A motel and ranch steakhouse. Kind of cool. Old, but cool. Not retro—the real thing.

"Where are we going?"

"You really getting an abortion?"

"I don't know."

"I thought maybe, maybe we'd get married."

"Huh? Don't be silly."

"Okay. But we'd have fun."

She hit him, but not too hard. "That's all boys think of. Isn't it?"

"I didn't mean that."

"Sure you did."

It was still a ways up the road. How long had he had this car out? A half hour? A half hour at least. "Not all," he said.

"The hell," she said. "That's all he wanted. He wanted to get me in my bed and plunge around in me with that big thing of his. That was the extent of what he wanted."

"Really."

"Yes, really. I'll tell you one thing. I didn't enjoy a minute of it."

"No?"

"No! There was no love in it. It was just him—getting off, if you know what I mean.'

"Yeah."

"I'll bet you do."

"Well," he said.

"I'm hungry."

"Well, sure. And we're stopping up ahead."

"Where? Not one of those X-rated places, I hope. He took me to one. That wasn't enough for him. You wouldn't believe."

"What?"

"Look, I'm going to flunk out. I know I am. And then where will I be? A fat flunk-out with a red-faced screaming baby."

"You fat?" He laughed. "Hey, don't you just love this machine?"

"How much did it cost? God, it must have cost a fortune. Did your dad buy it for you? Is he rich or something?"

"Naw."

He flicked his right-hand blinker on. He got on the off-ramp and cruised down the road, past dumpy little houses, sheds, and a caved-in ranch style house, a huge tree all over it.

"That's me, right there," she said. "Right there. That's where we'll live, won't we?"

"Us?"

"Just get that out of your head," she said.

"Um," he said. He gave her a quick look.

"I am so hungry."

✻ ✻ ✻

A bit later, he pulled into the Cock & Bull. It looked closed. And then he saw that it was closed. It had been a ranch steakhouse and motel.

"What is this?" she said. "What the hell?"

"Where I was hoping we could eat."

"Talk about a dump."

"It's closed."

"I'd say."

"Let's go."

"Where? I'm hungry."

"We've got to get back."

"You want me to starve?"

He remembered a place farther down this old road. It wasn't good, but it wasn't bad. It was another of those motels and ranch steakhouses. It had good tenderloin burgers and beer. And they hadn't checked ID's, at least the two or three times he'd been there.

"Let's go."

"Where?"

"A little ways."

"Okay. Okay."

She was quiet for a spell. And now and then he'd look over her way and desire her. She'd be his wife. They'd live above that old woman's room, and do it half the night and raise hell with that old prune-faced prude, and then he'd go off to work for Mr. Bulge, if he could swing that, and he'd come home to her, and they'd do it again. And then they'd watch TV or something. And maybe sometimes they go out drinking. Like now. And then they'd do it again.

He'd finish high school, of course. Sure.

"What are you thinking?" she said.

"I don't know."

"You do too."

"Of us," he said.

"Us? Are you kidding?"

"You like this car, don't you?"

"Not that much."

"Why not?"

"I'm getting an abortion. I can tell you that, right now. You can believe that if you believe anything."

"What's that like anyway? Is it painful?"

"How would I know?"

"I guess it depends on how big it is."

"You're stupid," she said. "Talking like that."

"I don't know anything about it."

"I'm starving. How many times do I have to say it?"

It was open. The Bronco. Another ranch motel and steakhouse. He had plenty of money on him, and he felt like splurging. He ordered a pitcher of beer, two tenderloins, and two large orders of fries.

They sat there, waiting. She looked perturbed. "What am I doing?" she said.

"Waiting. The food's good here—you'll see."

"What do I care about the food?"

"You like that car?"

"Yes. Yes. Why wouldn't I?"

"Want to see what it'll do?"

"If you want."

He took her by the hand. "You my girl?"

She jerked away. "No! I told you. I'm not and never will be your girl!"

He sat there, disconsolate. "You want that bastard

over me. That it?"

"I don't want anybody, least of all you."

"Abort it? Or put it up for adoption, huh?"

"How do I know? Don't bother me."

After another ten minutes, during which Lilac sat staring around the place and also excused herself to go to the ladies room, Frederick wondered about the car. Maybe he should call. It had been a good hour or so by now. And it was after 6 PM.

The food arrived. He dug in. She dug in. He ate ravenously. She ate ravenously. "Hungry, huh?" he said.

"I told you I was."

"You like it?"

She nodded. "Why wouldn't I?"

He waited a moment, then said, "What exactly do you have against me, anyway?"

She stopped eating. "What do I have for you?"

"I punched out that guy for you. That ought to count for something. And he's a mobster."

"Ha!"

"What?"

"He's no mobster. He's about as harmless as a baby rabbit."

"How do you know? How do you know such a thing?"

"I slept with him, you fool."

He stopped eating. "Huh? No. No you didn't. You didn't either. I don't care what—"

"What?"

"Never mind."

"Well, I did. He's a real bastard, I can tell you that. And I was sure he'd fixed me up good, too. And maybe he did."

"What do you mean?"

"Got me pregnant, idiot."

"Don't call me idiot."

"I didn't mean it. Don't take things so personally. The beer's good," she said, sipping. She smiled. She took his hand, held it momentarily, and then let loose.

"And the tenderloin," he said.

"I don't think you understand a thing about me," she said.

"Huh? Tell me, then."

"I want. I want lots of things, and here I am stuck with this"—she stuck her finger against her abdomen. "You think I want this?"

"His fault," said Frederick. "I'll bet he didn't use an ounce of protection."

"You think?"

"You mean you—"

"Men don't like rubbers. Need I say more?"

"No."

"Do they?"

"No."

"I'll bet you're a virgin and don't know the first thing about it."

"Yeah," he said.

"Yeah, what?"

"I've got to get back."

"Back where?"

"I've got to get back, but take your time. Eat. Enjoy."

"You're rather crazy," she said, smiling. "I kind of like that."

"Crazy how?"

"Oh, I don't know. I don't have to pin it down, do I?"

"No. I guess not."

She sighed. "I'd give anything. I mean anything. But I might as well take a gun and shoot myself."

"No. Don't talk like that."

"Then make me feel better."

❧ ❧ ❧

When he got her back to her house, she got out, didn't turn around and say anything, just took off for the front door.

He drove off for the car dealer.

It was 7:15 PM. He'd had that car out for over two hours. He entered the showroom, and a man, a different man, said, "Can I help you, sir?"

"I'm turning in that car out there. I took it out for a spin. I'm pretty much convinced—that's the car for me. You bet."

"You," he said. "Follow me, please."

The man was wearing a sports coat. A dark one. He wore a narrow tie. Brown.

"Okay," he said. "I'm sold on that car, I really am."

"You're in the buying mood, are you?" said the man, directing Frederick to a brown plastic chair, in front of his gray metal desk.

"That I am."

"You know, we just about called the authorities, but just in case you'd had an accident, run out of gas, got sick, and so forth, we delayed. What kept you so long?"

"Uh. Well, I couldn't seem to part with it. I confess to that. And then I got lost. Got really turned around. It was terrible, just terrible."

"Is that a fact?"

The man was drilling him with those blue eyes. "Where was this—where you got lost?"

"Off the interstate, on some abandoned road. I was trying to find my way back, but that wasn't the road to take. I'm sorry. I'm embarrassed."

"Is that right?"

"Yes, sir."

"So... you're a buyer. You're in the market."

"Yes, I am."

"How'd you like us to run your credit, then. Let's see what we can manage."

"Sure."

"Let me see your driver's license and one major credit card."

"I don't have a card."

The man stared at him. "We'll see. Wait here."

He sat there and watched the door, which the man had closed. He caught the time on the wall clock.

Suddenly the man was opening the door.

He sat down, with a file in his hand.

"Here's the thing. You'd have to have a co-signer. If you can manage that, the monthly payment would run you, with extras like an extended maintenance contract, right at nine-fifty a month for seven years. This is not a cheap car, sir. Do you have a co-signer?"

"Maybe."

The man nodded. "Uh huh. When can you obtain a signature from this co-signer?"

"Soon."

"All right. Come back in when you're ready. All right?"

"Yes, sir."

"I've got a man looking at the miles on that car. Wait here." He held a finger up. He left, closing the door.

Frederick sat there, debating.

The man came back with a sheet of paper. He held it up. "One hundred thirty-seven miles you put on that little red car. That's not acceptable. Not in the least. No one does that. You'll be buying that particular car if you decide to buy a car from Mason and Marks—which I certainly do advise." He held that same finger up. Come back with your co-signer. We'll expect you by tomorrow evening at this time. No later."

"Yes, sir."

"Now, I'll be needing this office." He pointed at the door.

Frederick nodded and rose. He made it to the door and outside. He had a considerable distance to walk.

6

"You want me to co-sign on a car loan," said Mr. Bulge. "What would possess you to think I'd ever consider such a thing? I'm your father's lawyer. Not your father."

"No, I know. But I can't see my father signing. I don't think he would. I'm sure he wouldn't."

"And you think I would."

"Would you?"

"Of course not. Now, then, have you rehearsed as I told you to?"

"No. Not really."

"Have or haven't?"

"Haven't."

"Then let's rehearse now. Why did you do it? What was the point? Did you conceptualize it?"

"I don't know. I didn't mean to. It just happened."

"No, no. The judge expects repentant behavior. Does that sound repentant to you?"

"No. But it's the truth."

"Sure it is. But maybe you should distort the truth a little bit. Just say something like: 'If I had this to do over, I would never, ever, have done what I did. Never, your honor. I plead for forgiveness. I am so, so guilty. I throw myself on the mercy of the court!' You see the difference?"

"But I'm not that guilty. He's a real bastard. That's what he is."

"He's out of that coma."

"Huh?"

"That's right."

"What do I do?"

"You've a few options. One: Make your court appearance, then make a quick getaway, never to appear in this city again. Two: Don't make the court appearance. I'll plead not guilty for you. Escape the city. The suburbs, the outlying rural areas! Three: Try to bribe this young man Dark to drop the case. But be sure you have a go-between. Don't, whatever you do, make the mistake of approaching the man on your own. He'll use a silencer. He'll not be averse to snuffing you out practically anywhere. Get my drift?"

"Then what do I do?"

"Go to court. Confess. Then in the witness box, let the judge know you're savvy. This man is a mobster. A monster. Point at him. Don't be afraid of accusatory behavior. Embarrass the man with his evil deeds."

"What evil deeds?"

"Don't you know?"

"No."

He shook his head. "I don't either." He rose from his office desk and parted the blinds that looked out onto the courthouse steps. "What did you think of my little missy?"

"Heather?"

"That's right."

"Nice."

"I'm sure the judge would love that."

"What?"

"The judge, you see, is a man without a woman. Well,

he's got a wife, but you know... you know how it goes. But if he were to have a woman of that caliber, I'm quite certain he could be persuaded. Understand?" He winked. He grinned.

"At five hundred an hour?"

"How did you know that?"

"She told me."

"Well, that's the starting rate. For the judge, I'm sure, knowing he's a deep pocket, she'd be charging more than that. I'd say prepare for twenty-five hundred an hour. At least."

"What?"

"A senator has to pay five thousand an hour. A governor ten thousand. One man running for president, the highest office in the land, paid twenty thousand. Imagine what a prince or king would have to pay."

"I don't have that kind of money."

"But you could arrange it, I expect. Half of it, perhaps."

"How?"

"You're looking at a year or more behind bars, given this particular judge. He's tough on crime."

Frederick thought about his cash. He thought about his lack of cash. Then he thought about that one spot midtown, GET YOUR BUCKS HERE. NO CREDIT CHECKS.

"I might be able to."

"Think of it as an investment. For a measly twelve hundred and fifty bucks, it's like you never did a thing at all. You don't even go to court. The judge drops the case for lack of evidence, or at least the prosecuting attorney does. And then you blow town."

"Um. Where to?"

"Or arm yourself."

"With what?"

"Something. Get a dog. A dog that bites. Lock your car in your garage."

"I have no car."

"What's a man without a car?"

"Twelve hundred and fifty?"

"You see, the judge likes my little missy. She used to work for him when she was but eighteen. He salivated over her. He still does. But he doesn't want to pay twenty-five hundred per hour. That's a pile. Twelve hundred and fifty? He might go for that. At least he'd go for five hundred—what's five hundred? In that case, your part's two thousand."

"But you said—"

"Mere speculation."

Frederick rose. "I've got to see about that car."

"The judge appreciates that—a man with a car. As long as it's a good one. Expensive. It's a measure of a man's character. See?"

❧ ❧ ❧

He was at the dealer again.

"What kind of a down would I need for that car—that red car?"

"You think you need to identify that car to me—as red versus blue or silver or tan or white? You think I've so easily forgotten your little escapade in that car?"

"No, sir."

"With a co-signer, no down needed. With no co-signer, a down of ten thousand dollars."

"Ten thousand."

"Dollars, young man."

"That much?"

"What were you thinking? A thousand, five hundred... two hundred?"

"I could swing two hundred."

The man laughed. A congested laugh, with a rattle to

it. He went through several throat clearings, and then he placed two hands on the desktop. He was a large man. He ran a finger over his pencil-line mustache. Then he sat back, lighting a cigar. "You'd have a heftier payment. Nothing comes free in this world, son. Didn't your daddy teach you that?"

"Yes, sir."

The man leaned over and placed some vinyl on the player. It kicked into action. It blew some notes. Jazzy notes, notes that made him want to get up and dance. He wanted to dance with Lilac. He wanted his hand around her narrow waist. He wanted to be elsewhere dancing with her.

The man was now keying in something on the computer.

He stopped and ran that same finger over his mustache. "Hmm." He clicked the keys and the printer went to work, and soon it was shooting out paper. The man went for it, stacked a sheaf of papers on his desk, and held it up to the light. "Thousand, twenty-five, seventy-eight a month, but that's with a long-term maintenance plan, and of course you've got to add insurance to that and general upkeep. The latter will be very inexpensive for the first year or so. The sales tax is figured in. And property tax—you won't have to worry about that for about a year and a half. Car insurance, though—at your age that could be costly."

"I thought it was nine hundred and something."

"Well, it's not." The man thumped his finger on the printout.

Frederick saw that he was now expected to say something. All he could think of was Lilac. All he could think of was that apartment over the old lady, and that made him cringe, but they'd just have to be quiet. The only thing was, could you be that quiet with such passion, such pleasure? And then he wondered what "that quiet" amounted to.

"I'll take it," he said.

"You will? Well, then, I'll signal the boys out there to do the detailing on it. Attempting as much as they can to make it look like it's brand new—in spite of the fact that it's not."

"I'll sign," said Frederick. "You give me the papers and I'll sign."

"Sure you will. Don't you know the first thing about comparison shopping? Well, I guess you gave it a real go out there, and you fell in love—is that it?"

"Yes, sir."

"Um hum. You find a place in the lounge out there, grab yourself a cola, and meanwhile I'll work up the sales contract."

"Yes, sir."

The man laughed. "I'm supposed to be the one saying 'Yes, sir'—not you!"

"Yes, sir."

The man shook his head. He pointed at the door and said, "Please shut it. And thank you."

"Yes, sir."

The man shook his head.

Frederick sat in the lounge, sipping a cola. He wished he had a cigarette, but he'd never smoked. He'd never felt right doing that. For one thing, he didn't like the smell of it, and second, he worried he'd die of lung cancer at forty or fifty. He didn't want to die of lung cancer. He didn't want to die of a motorcycle accident either, and when he thought of motorcycles, he generally thought of crashing into something. Sometimes it was a car, sometimes a tree, once it was a train. And he pictured his whole body run over by those steel wheels, cutting him in half. He also thought of deep ditches, and flying right into them—what that would do to his body. Dead. You'd be dead. He didn't want that. Who did?

Well, anyway, he'd be getting his red sports car for a thousand or so a month. With an extended warranty, though it was in good shape now, but later it would wear down, just like everything did. Like his dad's second car. He remembered when that was brand new, shiny. That red car was shiny, he'd keep it shiny, and somehow he'd pay for it. He'd get good work with Mr. Bulge, right out of high school, you bet.

It was about a half hour when the man poked his head in the doorway. "All set."

"Good!"

"All right. Now the law requires full disclosure, so I'm going to go over each and every aspect of this sales contract with you."

And he did.

It was difficult to listen to, but Frederick got the gist. The main thing was that the first payment was due in forty-five days. It would be early spring. How much would Lilac be showing by then?

"Here's the keys. The keys to the kingdom, as it were."

"Thanks." He didn't want to sound too happy. He was, but he didn't want to sound that way.

"Off we go," said the man. "You're the proud owner of one fine car, such as it is. Worn a little but detailed to our company's best specifications."

"Oh, thank you," said Frederick.

"I suppose I should be the one thanking you," said the man. And then a grim look. "Don't miss a payment. They swoop down on that sort of thing. It gets ugly. Real ugly."

"No, no," said Frederick.

He drove out of the lot. Soon he was on his way to Lilac Johnson's.

But he'd have to stop for gas. Damn. They didn't even fill it.

7

The front door opened almost as soon as he'd knocked. There stood Lilac's father in jeans and tee-shirt. "Yes? Yes? What can I do for you?"

He pointed. "See?"

"I see, so come on in. Yes, do come in. What are we up to, exactly? Have you made the arrangements? Have you secured the services of a minister? She's showing, you might have noticed. Not much, but... ah, a little. It's... well it's a shame that... what I'm trying to say," said Lilac's father, leading him through the living room into the kitchen, "is that we must make haste. Well, I don't mean haste in the sense that 'Haste makes waste'—but promptness. That's it. Promptness. 'Readiness is all,' as the bard said."

"What are you saying to him?" said Lilac. She, too, was in a tee-shirt with her ample bosom making it bulge out, and Frederick was caught trying not to look.

"I'm saying that something must be done, and it must be done in a hurry. Are you going to the prom?" he asked Frederick.

"I've got my red car out there, and if you'd like to go with me—somewhere—that would be pleasant."

"For you, but what about me?"

"You don't like my car?"

"I see you looking at me. Go ahead and say it. Pregnant. Isn't that the word?"

"Him," said Frederick.

"I don't want him. I'm breaking it off."

"Because he's a bastard?"

"No, silly. My child will be the bastard. Like I care."

"I'll marry you," he said. "Come with me, be my bride, and we—"

"Will all the pleasures prove?" said her father. "A fine plan!"

"I don't want to!" She backed up a few steps. She grabbed the door frame.

"Oh, well... you don't have to," said Frederick.

"I don't want to marry anybody or talk about it. What I don't want more than marrying anybody is talking about it!"

"We've done some considerable talking," said her father.

"I'd just like, I'd just like—to rid myself of this thing! This horrid thing!"

"Oh," said her father. "Well, that is one way. One has to reflect on such a thing."

"I'm going with you," she said, taking Frederick's arm. "Take me out of here now!"

"I only meant to help you formulate a plan," said her father. "A plan with a structure. A well-structured plan, as it were."

"He's an idiot!" cried Lilac. "Let's go."

"What about your coat?" said her father. "I'll go get it."

"Yes, yes," she said.

He wished it was spring so she wouldn't have to cover up her ample bosom with that coat.

She was now getting it on.

Then they were arm in arm, moving through the living area to the front door.

"My, my," said her father, strolling along.

"See," said Frederick, when she had opened the front door. "Right out there waiting for us!"

"How are you paying for that?" said her father.

"Sir?"

"Don't call my father 'sir'. Let's go."

They were out the door now, and they were still arm in arm, moving toward his new red car. The orange sun was descending in a brilliant wall of blue.

❧ ❧ ❧

"Don't you think it's a beauty?" he inquired as he sped along the interstate.

"Um," she said.

A call came in on his cell.

"Um."

"Better answer that, hadn't you?"

"While I'm driving?"

"I'll answer it."

"No. I'll call back."

She read the number off the screen.

"That's my lawyer. Get that," he said, motioning at the screen.

She did, and Frederick said, "Hi," with his eyes on the flatbed truck ahead of him, in the middle lane.

"Frederick, you poor man, how is it?"

"Good! But—"

"The judge says he'll get it dismissed. Are you in a private area? Can we talk?"

"Well." It was loud and clear, on the screen.

"Okay, then, the judge is a man of great needs—"

"No, I can't. No!"

"Oh, well, then. I'll text you. How is that?"

"Yes, sir."

A laugh on the other end. "That missy!"

And then the screen went blank.

"What's going on?" said Lilac.

"Huh?"

"That judge. What's going on?"

"Not much."

"You paying him off?"

"Uh—no."

"Sure you are."

"I am?"

"You know you are and you should. Why take a chance? How much are you paying him?"

"Uh, well. I've forgotten."

"Forgotten? How could you forget a thing like that?"

"I don't know. It's privileged information. I'm not allowed to talk about it. Or even think about it."

"Well, screw you, then. A husband always tells his wife."

"Husband?"

"Who knows?"

She was quiet for the longest time as he raced through the interstate traffic. Husband, wife. Those words churned in him. After a while, they were in the country.

"Where are we going, anyway?"

"You want to eat?"

"Yes, I do. It's like I can't get enough."

"Steakhouse?"

"Okay. I guess."

He thought of that motel. The Bronco Ranch Motel and Steakhouse.

"We'll be there in a minute. Or soon, anyway."

"Well, I don't know," she said. "That judge is pretty mean from what I've heard."

"Yeah?"

"So you'd best pay him off. It's the only way these days. That's the way it's done."

"It is?"

"Give them what they want. And it doesn't have to be money."

"Oh."

"Don't act like you don't know."

"No, I know. Sure."

"That Horatio Dark?"

"Yes?"

"I'm glad you clobbered him, but sorry he's after you now. Well, not him, but one of his cohorts."

"Huh?"

"You don't think he'd have cohorts? Sure he does. He used to beat up people a few years back when he was seventeen, but now he lets others, made men like him, do the job."

"How old is he?"

"Twenty. Twenty-one."

"Yeah. And dumb fuck's still in high school."

"That's right. He had to repeat two or three years. This year he graduates or that's it for him."

"No diploma."

"Oh, they'll give him a diploma."

"Huh?"

"I'm sooo hungry."

"Just a few miles."

"Well, it had better be."

When they arrived at the Bronco, a maroon car was roaring its engine with tough looking guys leaning out of open windows, with cigarettes dangling out of their mouths.

They pulled ahead, blocking him. One man suddenly got out and was signaling Frederick.

"What?" he said.

"You know what. They look bad," said Lilac. "Real bad."

And then the man was going for his trunk. The lid

popped up. He was bringing out a tire iron. And now he was heading their way.

"No," said Frederick.

He backed up fast, shooting gravel. That hooligan running, sprinting, the tire iron swinging. His cigarette drooping out of his mouth. It looked like it was stuck to his lips.

That's when he saw it: a black object, flying toward him, twisting in the air. And then a loud banging on his hood.

He yelled. She yelled.

But he was on the road now. There was another ranch motel and steakhouse not too far off, but he couldn't remember the name.

Lilac next to him, she was crying, sobbing. "He ruined our car! It'll never be the same!"

"Our?"

"Oh, hush!"

Ours.

"What're you thinking?"

"I'll get it fixed, you bet."

"You've got insurance—but what if you didn't?"

"Sure." He nodded. And then it hit him. He didn't have it. He'd forgotten to get it. But how'd he know he'd be vandalized as soon as he got the car out on the road?

"God, I hope so."

The land was rising, with hills and bluffs looking down on the brown river. Sometimes he could see it; sometimes he couldn't.

"There's another steakhouse down the road a little way," he said.

"Oh, is there?"

"Yep."

And suddenly he remembered the name. The Last Roundup.

He rolled into the lot of the Roundup. It was 1950s style like the other one. Not retro, just old. The real thing. A long, clapboard motel with about twenty rooms. Needed some paint, but oh, well.

A few cars sat in the lot.

He got out. She got out.

He looked at the hood. Big dent and considerable abrasion. This would cost hundreds of dollars.

"That's got to be three or four thousand bucks," said Lilac, fingering it.

"Damn! I hope not." Was he about to cry?

She laid a hand on his. "It's okay. It'll be okay."

"I have no insurance."

"Huh?"

"I forgot."

"Well, hell," she said. She was marching toward the steakhouse.

He moved fast and took her by the hand. She let him.

He grabbed a table close to the window, which looked out on the parking lot—and his poor red car.

The waitress showed up. They were the only ones there.

"I want a lot," said Lilac, staring at the menu.

He wondered if he had any money on him. He didn't want to pull out his billfold just now, but it struck him that he might have left most of what he had back at the apartment in one of his clothes drawers. Most of it, but perhaps not all of it?

"I'll take French fries," he said.

"That's all?"

"For starters."

"Oh, okay, if that's what you want. A cheeseburger," she said. "French fries. Chocolate malt. Cherry pie. That's it." She glanced at him.

The waitress was writing it down. She looked dangerously thin. Meth?

He went for his billfold. He got it in his lap and tried to get a quick look.

"You don't have to pay till later," said Lilac.

There was but one dollar in his billfold. And then it struck him that he'd left five dollars in the glove compartment—money left over from gas.

"Got to run. Back in a minute."

"Restroom?"

"Outside."

"What?"

"Car."

"Why?"

"Because. Back in a minute."

"Well, hell."

He got inside his red car, in the glove compartment, and grabbed the five. Then he slipped it into his billfold.

Inside, there she was, with a look. "What was so important?"

"Oh, nothing."

"It's something. You can't fool me."

"I've got six dollars," he said. "And that's it."

"So?"

"That's not enough. It'll be more than that."

"Don't look at me."

"What'll we do? What?"

"What'll *you* do?"

"I... don't know."

"Give them the six and stiff them for the rest. It can't be that much."

"You think that'll work?"

"It has other times."

"Huh? What? When?"

"Like when my boyfriend did it. That's when."

"Oh."

The waitress delivered their food. They took their time. They ate. He worried. Would they arrest him? Decking that Dark guy and now this? First assault, now theft?

After a little while, she said, "I'm finished."

"Okay," he said.

She raised her hand and the waitress was coming. "You're supposed to do that," she said, "but since you didn't, I had to."

"You didn't give me—"

"You all ready for your bill?"

"Yes," said Frederick.

He waited. Lilac was grinning.

The waitress tore it off a pad. He looked. It was $11.73.

He went for his six dollars. He handed the money to the waitress. "I'm sort of... short," said Frederick.

"Eleven seventy-three."

"I can send the rest later."

"That won't work. And if you don't pay up, they'll think I took it. It being cash."

"What do you want me to do? I don't have it."

"Get it," said the waitress.

"Where?"

She looked at Lilac.

"I don't have it."

"I'll check with the manager." She moseyed off.

Lilac got up. "Quick!"

"Huh?"

"Quick!"

She shot toward the exit. He followed.

They hurried out to the lot.

"Fast," she said when they got in the car.

"Um," he said. Then he tore out. Lilac was looking out the open window.

"Everything okay?" he said.

"Perfect," she said.

# 8

He was heading back to the Bronco. He was with Lilac in his red sports car with its hood severely damaged, and he wondered how he'd make the first payment, and whether or not Mr. Bulge would hire him, and what he'd do without money to pay for the car and the rent—and what about that judge and that Missy?

"You caught up in something?"

"What?"

"Something?"

"Something what?"

"Are you caught up—oh, never mind."

"I'm just thinking," he said.

"About what?"

"Getting back."

"Well, hell."

He wished he could get a motel for the two of them at the Bronco, but how would he pop the question?

"We've got to be a hundred miles from home."

"Sixty. Or so."

"Is that right?"

"Yep—trip thing here says it is."

He was circling around a densely forested bluff right

now, and below them that brown river, which from here he could barely see. Just a thicket of tall, leafless trees. Bare. The winter depressed him. He needed a woman to keep him warm. And other things.

"I hope you score. With that judge, I mean. Otherwise, you'll probably spend a year in county lockup. Unless Horatio Dork gets you."

"Dark."

"Well, he's Dork to me. You're better than him. Not much better, but better."

"Really?"

"Just leave it there," she said.

When they came to the Bronco, the lot was clear—no maroon car.

He pulled into the gravel lot and parked right in front of the restaurant picture window, through which he could see a man and a woman, raising beers, blowing smoke.

Those two oldsters were now gazing out the window at them. The man, wearing a brown cowboy hat, was waving. The woman was frowning.

"I don't like this place," said Lilac.

He was looking at the motel. Seventy-two fifty a night. He could write a check. It might bounce, but he'd cover it —somehow.

"What's the problem?"

He couldn't help it. It had all been moving in this direction. All along, at least for him, this is where it had been going. He'd punched that Dark guy out, standing up for his girlfriend—who wasn't his girlfriend at the time, but was really, actually, his girlfriend, give it time. He'd been courting her as best he could. Bought this red car, and here they were.

"What's the problem? You moving or not?"

Those faces in the window. Old. Gnarled fingers clutching those dark bottles.

"What I'm thinking," he said. "What I've been

thinking, I mean. I don't mean anything bad by it, but what I've been thinking... you know how it is... with guys, I mean. You know."

His hand went to hers and clasped it.

She jerked it away. "What! What the hell?"

He tried to smile. "I didn't mean anything—not really. I didn't mean anything at all."

"Oh? Is that right?" She pointed at the motel. "That looks like a real dump. I'll bet there's black widow spiders in the bed. Bed bugs. I'll bet you'd die in that place."

"We could get a better place. A lot better than this. There's places off the interstate. You know, some nice places. Cool places with hot tubs."

She was staring at him. "What do you think I am—a whore?"

"No. No, no."

"Well, you sure act like it. Why'd I want to shack up with you?"

He wanted to say: "Because you're already pregnant and I'm almost your husband—that's why." But he didn't say that. He hemmed and hawed some, and then he said. "We could have a good time. It could be fun."

She laughed. It was a spiteful one. "What you think is fun isn't what I think is fun. I don't particularly want a man all over me, doing this and doing that. Let's go. I'll scream if you don't. And I mean it!"

Those two sitting in the steakhouse were now tapping their beers on the window. He couldn't hear it, but he saw what was happening there. They felt like they were on display. But he felt like it was he and Lilac, they were the ones on display.

And then he saw that car. That maroon car.

Heard it first, with an engine squealing, screeching, shrieking, and then saw it, blasting over the gravel, the rocks flying, spitting.

He put it in drive and hit the gas. He got down the

road a little way. He saw Lilac turning her head, looking back.

"See them?"

"No. Thank God."

They were flying along back toward home now, and they'd be back by dark. And then maybe, maybe, he could get her in his place, and maybe he could get her in bed, and maybe they'd make the bedsprings sing. He couldn't keep from thinking about it.

"You're awfully quiet," she said.

"Oh. I don't mean to be."

"You're pissed, aren't you?"

"Huh?"

"Yes, you are. Because you want it, and I won't give it to you. That's the way it is with men. You don't give it to them, and they get pissed. Just like that. Wham."

"I'm not pissed."

"Yes, you are. Men always are. They want it every minute. Girls don't want it every minute, but guys do. It's like they're obsessed with it. That's not normal. Maybe you don't know that, but it's not."

"But for guys, it's normal, huh?'

"It's not normal. It's pathological."

"Really!"

"You know what that means?"

"Sure."

"I doubt it."

He'd heard of it at least. He nodded.

"You don't make very good grades, do you?"

"Huh? Sometimes."

"In which classes?"

"Some—like math. I'm pretty good in math."

"What grades?"

"C's. And that's not bad in math."

"Well, it's not good either."

He felt like his head was going in circles. He made D's

in Spanish, C's in Geography, C's in English, and B's a few times in History. He mentioned the latter.

"I suppose that's good. But me, I make almost nothing but A's and B's—with the preponderant outcome being A's."

"Preponderant?"

"You don't know what that word means?"

"Sure."

"Yeah, I'll just bet."

He felt his hand being clasped, and then gripped. He looked over. She was smiling.

He chalked it up. He'd remember that. How she was smiling, and he was smiling back.

❧ ❧ ❧

He pulled the red car in his parking space. He sat there.

"This is my place," he said. "Thought you might like to see it."

"You thought you'd get me in bed is what you thought."

"No, no. No. Of course not."

"Yes, you did. Take me home. I've done enough of that stuff for a year. Look at my tummy."

He looked at it. It didn't appear to be bulging yet, but maybe soon—if she was pregnant at all. Was she?

"Okay," he said.

"If you won't try anything, I'll give it a look," she said.

"Sure."

"You say that an awful lot. Say something else. And don't answer me 'Sure.'"

"Okay."

"That's not much better."

He got out of the car, and she was getting out. And then they were both heading up the outside steps, him leading her because after all, he was the one with the key.

❦ ❦ ❦

A knocking on the door. He saw who it was in the glass window of the door.

He got up off the bed, leaving her lying there, fully clothed. He wasn't going to get anywhere tonight.

He went to the door, opening it a crack.

"Let me in. Who is that?"

"A friend... just a friend."

He opened the door, and the old woman stepped in.

"Friend, my eye. You," she pointed, "you get out of here. And now!" Gesticulating with bony fingers.

"I am Lilac Johnson, is who I am."

"So? Get thee hence."

"What?"

"Get thee hence. Pack up, leave. You are not to be in this boy's room."

"Yeah? Who do you think you are, anyway? I'll visit him just as much as I please. Whenever I want. You don't have a thing to do with it. You think you're some sort of moral police? The vice squad?"

"Out. Out now!"

"What I'm about to do, right now, is take off all of my clothes and see what you say then. How would you like that?"

The landlady stood there. Her eyebrows squinched up. She looked at her, then at him, then at her. "Well, I—"

"I'm going to start right now!" shouted Lilac.

"I'll have a word with you later," said the landlady, shaking a finger, and soon he could hear her on the outside stairs. Clunk. Clunk. Clunk. Down, down, down.

He looked at Lilac.

"Were you really, were you going to—"

"Are you serious? I've got to leave."

9

When he dropped her off, he went straight back to his place and lay down. He could hear the landlady down below, making stirring and rumbling noises.

He fell asleep after a while, awoke at seven, dressed, and by eight he was at Bulge's office. He was missing homeroom, but who cared? He didn't.

"Judge threw it out. That's official. I'll need fifteen hundred by bank closing time this evening."

"Huh? I don't have fifteen hundred."

"It's between you and the judge. I don't give much of a fig. He does, though."

"Where would I get fifteen hundred anyway?"

"Loan company. Loan shark. No bank's going to touch it. Unless you've got collateral. Do you?"

"What if I... what if I mentioned the judge?"

"Judge? You might, but I wouldn't."

"But he's the one that needs the money."

"True. Mention his name. That'd be good. He's the one in need here. You have an appointment, a rendezvous with you-know-who?"

"No."

"Well, then."

"What?"

"You're not responsible for the judge's... lust, to put it plainly."

"But you swung a deal for me. Didn't you?"

"You wish to live up to the terms of the contract?"

"No—unless I have to."

"No contract signed. It was verbal. Of course if you don't fork over the fifteen hundred—in cash—by this evening, bank closing time, I wouldn't ever appear in the judge's court. That would not be advisable."

"Court?"

"No one ever intends to—take it from me, a lawyer."

"You mean—"

"I mean you're going along just fine, and suddenly there you are standing in front of the judge. It's like a bad dream. Do you intend to dream a bad dream? No, I doubt you do. Do you intend to dream that there are no toilets in a building, or that there is one, but it's in a public place? With a half dozen or more onlookers? No, I doubt you do. Same with the judge, son, there you are just like in a building with no toilets and you have a fierce need to go."

"But why? Why?"

"Who knows why? A lawyer deals with stratagems on how to get out of problems. The rest is the work of spooks, or some sort of fate or determinism. Do you believe in fate? Do you believe in determinism? They're different, you know. You're a cog in the causal chain. Unless—unless, it's a matter of intent. Did you, or do you, intend to defraud the poor judge?"

"No, no, of course not."

"I'd fork over the fifteen hundred, then."

"But I don't see how I can get it."

"Good point. Good point. And why should you?"

"What?"

"Well, what's the judge done for you? Nothing big,

really. Got one more item off his docket. He cleared a space for a little me-time. What's it to him? Of course he was a-hungering for you-know-who, but who doesn't hunger now and then? Let him suck it up. Let him pay the entire four to five thousand per hour. What's money anyway?"

"I fear, though," said Frederick.

"Sure you do, and why wouldn't you? Having a judge like that after you."

"I'm getting the money!"

"Wait, now. Don't be foolish. Or too foolish."

"Am I, though? Who wants a judge after him? Not me. I don't want a judge after me."

"No one does, but what can he do, really? It'll be up to the jury. And the prosecuting attorney."

"What will be?"

"The next time you appear in court."

"I'm not appearing in court!"

"Well, then, good day to you."

He started to leave. "But I could use a job. Of some sort."

"Like what?"

"Anything. Practically anything. Just so long as it's after school—and on the weekends."

"Um hum. You don't ask for much, do you? Well, I'll be thinking."

"You think you do have—"

"Did I say that? I'll be thinking—that's what I said, didn't I now?"

"Yes, sir."

"Okay, then come back tomorrow or the next day, or perhaps next week, or next month, and we'll see."

"Good!"

"Don't count those chickens."

❧ ❧ ❧

Lilac's was the next stop. He wasn't about to go for that dough for the judge—not yet anyway. He was there in ten minutes, pulling up along the curb, next to that tree. When he got out, he stood looking at the hood. It was banged up pretty bad. It looked worse every time he looked at it. It would cost a lot. But how could he not spend the money?

He wasn't even to the door when it opened wide—and there stood Lilac.

"What do you want?"

"You. If I could."

"Me. You think you can have me? With a beaten-up car like that? I don't go with guys with bad cars."

"It's not a bad car. I'll vacuum it out, too, and it'll look just like new."

"Yeah. With what that guy did with that tire iron. You think so, do you?"

"I couldn't help that."

"Who says you could? But why'd you stop in that horrible place?"

"I want you. That's why."

"Oh, well, that's a proposal."

"But I do. I want to right now."

"Like in being married?"

"Yes!"

"Not out here you're doing that. I don't marry any man at my door. You think I'd say yes to a proposition like that?"

"Then let me in."

"No."

"Please. I want in."

"I'll just bet you do."

"Please."

"Come on in. Come in. I don't know what's got into me to let the likes of you in my house. But come in."

"Why do you hate me so?" asked Frederick. There was mournful twang to his voice, and he immediately regretted it.

"I don't hate you, and quit whining."

He was whining because he had to have Lilac. If there was a girl in the entire world he needed, it was Lilac Johnson.

"Come sit," she said.

He followed her. He felt like a puppy.

"There," she said, directing him to a sofa. She patted the pillow, and then she made her way to a love seat, directly across from him.

"I want to marry you," he said. "I really want to marry you."

"I know. I heard it the first time. You want to sleep with me. Your landlady's right about that, and if you think you're putting me to bed there, you can just forget it. Nobody's putting me to bed in a place like that."

"Why not?"

"You have to ask?"

"Yes—why?"

"It stinks. And besides that, the bed's lumpy."

"Stinks?"

"Yes. It does."

He sat forward. "If I had a better place?"

"You think that's all I'm interested in? A better place?"

"Well."

She settled her eyes on him, those blue, twinkling eyes. "I like a nice, big, roomy apartment, carpeted, fully furnished. I like modern kitchen appliances. I like a big King-size bed. With a mattress that isn't lumpy or out of shape or sunken in. I like a man who'll make me feel like a million bucks."

Her voice had raised. Her eyes were shining bright.

There was a strident, febrile air about her that fascinated but also frightened him. He debated it. He struggled. "What... what would a place like that cost?"

"I don't like that question!"

"Oh."

She again settled her eyes on him. "Probably fifteen hundred to two thousand a month, at least."

"Damn," he said.

"Well, hell," she said. "Get the picture?"

"Yes, I do. But a high school student—a senior, I mean —how can a guy like that afford a place like that?"

"He can't, stupid."

"I'm not stupid," said Frederick. "Don't call me stupid." And there, again, that whiny voice.

"Oh, don't be so easily offended!" She gave him a sly smile, her lower lip folded over perfectly white teeth. "Were you to marry me, I'd have to have a place like that. I can just imagine it. A hot tub. All the luxuries. I can just feel them, see them, touch them!"

She looked off in space for the longest time. Where was she?

He must pull her back in. "Uh," he said. "What are you thinking?"

"What, think," she said.

"My place costs one hundred and seventy-five a month," he said, "which I can ill afford."

"Ha! I like that 'ill afford'? Where'd you get that?"

"Oh, I don't know. I read a lot." He didn't, but it suddenly came to him to say that.

"Yeah, well. If you want me—and my baby—you've got to be a good provider. That's what you've got to be. Bottom-line: I don't like junk. I detest junk. If there's anything I hate, it's junk. Junk this, junk that. It's like some big burden! Like get rid of it! Now!"

Her eyes had grown large. She was huffing.

"But my car's not junk," he murmured.

"Now it is. After you let that thug bang it up like that. Why didn't you get out and do something about it? Why'd you let that scum beat the living daylights out of that new car? That beautiful baby? That top-of-the line beauty?"

"You do like it, then?"

"Not beaten to death, I don't."

"No, I understand. I don't either."

"Fix it. Right away."

"I don't have any insurance—like I said."

"Uh huh. How many times have you said that? What's that to me?"

"I just... want you," he said. "I just want—"

She rose from the love seat. "Well, maybe I don't want you! Unless you meet certain conditions. Expectations. Got that?"

"Conditions."

"And expectations. Do I have to spell it out? Again?"

He still sat there, looking up at her. "Do you... sort of like me? Sort of?"

She smiled. "Maybe. Maybe I do. Will you get that car fixed? Will you get that apartment?"

He rose. "Yes, I will!"

"Good, then," she said. "Oh, good." She came for him and wrapped her arms around him, and her voice grew soft and whispery as she said, "I could... in a car like that and a place like that. I could. I'd want to. A girl doesn't like bad stuff. She likes good stuff. And... would you wear some men's cologne?"

"Yes," he murmured. "For sure."

She backed away. "There's a body shop down the road, about six blocks."

"Okay," he said.

"See about that, please," she said.

10

YOU WRECK IT—WE FIX IT!

He pulled into the gravel lot. A guy in an orange tee-shirt was doing something to the underside of a black truck. "Yep," he said.

"My red sports car, it got banged up."

The man gave him a look. It wasn't condemning, but what was it? Frederick felt ill at ease. The man came around. Took a look. Stood there. "How'd that happen?"

"A guy took a tire iron to it."

"Umm. Is that a fact?" The guy in the orange tee-shirt let out a few epithets. "He sure did. This'll cost you, especially being a new car—and an expensive one. Vandalism. Your insurer will go after that party. Do you know his name?"

"No. Not at all."

"How's that? Down in the bad part of the city? Was it there?"

"No, it's about fifty miles from here. Off the interstate. Some dump of a place. He came out swinging. He threw it just as I was exiting the lot."

"Well, now."

"But I don't have insurance."

"What? On a new car like this?"

"No. I forgot to call."

"Well, you'd have it on the way home from the dealer—I

think. If you've got other cars insured. Sure, you would. You live over in those parts?"

"No."

"Damn."

"I can't live with this," said Frederick. "My girlfriend... you know—"

"Doesn't want to ride in a junk heap, huh? What girl would?"

"It's not a junk heap, is it?"

"Well, it sure don't look all that good." He pawed it, eyed it. "It's getting close, to be honest with you. Only this is coming from a body shop man. So..." He cracked a smile.

"Um."

"Come on in, and we'll get an estimate, and see what this is going to do to your wallet."

Frederick followed him in. Look at the arms on that guy. He had to work out. Sure he did.

He sat there in an orange plastic chair for about fifteen minutes, and then the guy in the orange tee-shirt ripped off a page from a pad he'd been working on and slid it Frederick's way. It had that logo at the top: You Wreck It —We Fix It!

He got a quick look at the figuring and then the total.

Eighteen hundred, fifty-seven dollars, and forty-three cents.

"I'd go after that vandal," said the guy in the orange tee-shirt. "Get the police on his tail."

"Yeah."

"Make him pay that," he motioned at the form, "and more. For emotional pain."

"Emotional?"

"Sure. You damned right. Doesn't it hurt to look at it?"

"Yeah."

"Well, now."

❧ ❧ ❧

He called Lilac.

"Yes, yes, what do you want?"

He said it.

"You think I'm going out there with you to get beaten on the head with a tire iron?"

"No. But I need help. I need to find that hooligan."

"So?"

"To make him pay."

"Oh, yeah, you're going to make him pay."

"I'll take him to court. I'll nail him for vandalism."

"Sure you will."

"You coming—with me?"

"No."

"Please."

"No."

"I'll... get that apartment," he said. "I'll sue him for a million bucks. I'll sue all of them!"

"Are you serious?"

"I am serious."

"I'm not getting bashed in the head with a tire iron."

"I could maybe get Dark to go. He's big. He's tough. He's a criminal."

A pause. Noises on the phone. "My god, you mean that?"

"Yes."

"Why would he do that? What's in it for him?"

"I don't know. At least he's out of that coma."

"Put him in another one?"

"I'm going to ask him."

"I'll go," she said. "Just don't ask Dork."

"Dark."

"No, it's Dork. At least you stood up to him. You're my hero on that score."

"Really?" He said it under his breath. He could hardly believe it.

⁂

"I don't know why I'm going with you."

"When we get there, we look for those hooligans."

"I'm not looking for any hooligans. Maybe you are, but I'm not."

"They're not so tough. Not without their tire irons."

"You think they won't have tire irons? Is that what you think?"

"I'm not allowing a punk to ruin my red little baby."

"What about your woman?"

This struck him. "You really are? You really are my woman?"

"No. Not really. I just said that. I don't know what I am. Not really. I'm sick, sick, sick of everything. You'd better get that apartment if you want me to be your woman."

He grasped her hand.

She pulled away.

"Please," he said. And took her hand again.

She let him.

⁂

It was sixty-two miles down, or up, the road. He clocked it from the on-ramp to the interstate, on Masters Drive. There they sat in the red car. In front of the Bronco Motel and Steakhouse.

She was fidgeting. "I hope they don't show up."

"But they've got to."

"You're awfully brave. I like a brave man."

"I just want to see them. I want to confront them. I want to—beat them up."

"All of them?"

"Him. That bastard."

"You better watch it," she said. "You might have gotten Dork, but them? They're different. They're worse."

"Than a mobster?"

"Some mobsters."

At that, he heard a noise. A whistling of some kind, a grinding, a shrieking. A whining underneath all that. The springs singing? Because yes, it was that maroon car. The windows were down, and that hooligan was shaking his fist, laughing.

"I'm getting out," said Frederick.

And then a tire iron was swinging out the opened window.

"You'll get killed!"

He stepped out of the car, stood there. That hooligan, with dirty yellow teeth, half of them missing, got out too. There was something in the movement of those legs, that torso, that head swinging.

He was on his way over. Kicking rocks. He stooped over and he flung a rock. It hit the window of his red car. "Hey!" Frederick cried.

And then he was there—that hooligan. Direct confrontation. This was a man-to-man encounter. This was what you daydreamed about at night before you fell asleep and dreamed. It wasn't real. But it was.

"You wanting trouble, son?"

"I want two thousand bucks—is what I want."

The guy stepped forward with his tire iron. He bent over Frederick's red car as though inspecting it carefully for bug spots. He ran one hand smoothly over the brilliant red surface, lingering over the damage, that big dent, with the awful abrasion, which broke Frederick's heart.

"Tell you what, I got a hood that'll fit this baby pretty nicely. I'll even put it on for you—different color, black, but still it's a hood."

"Fork over two thousand," said Frederick, watching that tire iron.

The hooligan raised the tire iron and grinned. It was a nasty one. And then he came down on the hood with a smash. And then another. And then another. Frederick stood looking. He didn't want to look, but he couldn't help but look. He felt his heart, or some organ, accelerating in his chest to his throat.

He started to go for this hooligan, but the tire iron was swinging this way and that. Up and down, and all around.

Finally, the man with bad teeth gave it one more bad one. And then he approached Frederick. "Want your whole car to look like that?"

It was one bad mess of smashed metal. Bumpy, like red blisters. Like pustules. It was a red car with leprosy. It was a sick, sick car.

He shot a look at the maroon car. No license plate. "No."

"Okay, then. Leave me alone, son."

"I'm not your son," said Frederick. He took out his cell phone, tapped his camera, and aimed it at the hooligan. And then he started with the shots.

The hooligan rushed him, but Frederick took off. He ran straight for the Bronco Steakhouse.

He felt hands grabbing at his coat. But he pulled the door open and kicked back. He was inside. The hooligan had backed off. Outside he could see the other hooligans approaching his red car—and Lilac inside it.

No, no!

He called 911.

Now that hooligan was back at the car, beating at the glass with that tire iron.

Frederick was trying to explain who he was and where he was when the passenger side window got a bad one and glass was smashing and falling out.

Lilac!

He ran straight for his car. He could see: she was moving over. She was taking the wheel. Another hooligan was crashing in her window. Fast, she was digging out. Fast, she was spitting gravel.

Then hooligans were heading for that maroon car.

❧ ❧ ❧

He waited and waited, pacing over the gravel, and finally he spotted his little red car making the bend in the road and entering the lot.

He hurried toward it.

She got out.

She stood there.

"You," he said. "You!"

"Dear god, I thought I was a goner. And you, you abandoned me. Why? Why would you do that?"

"He was chasing me with that tire iron."

"So, he was beating my window in!"

"I called—I called 911."

"Oh, whoopee."

"How far did they follow you?"

"I'll bet you'd like to know."

He nodded.

Because it had been a half hour or more since he'd seen her zooming out of the Bronco lot.

"Five, ten miles. I got off the road where they couldn't see me."

"Um—good."

"I guess you'd just leave me in that car to be murdered."

"No, no." But wasn't it true? Hadn't he? "I had to call 911, didn't I? I had to do that."

"So? Where are they?"

"I don't know."

She was getting in on the passenger's side. Her window was caved in. But so was his.

"If you can't get 911 for this, you can't get them for any-thing," she said. "And I mean it."

"Well, I'm not giving up."

"This car is a loss. It's totaled. It makes me sick to look at it."

And then, suddenly he spotted them again, that maroon car racing into the lot, hitting pot holes, leaping, bounding.

He hit the gas pedal. He tore past them, and he was on the road again. Heading back.

In his rearview mirror, he saw that maroon car. Getting closer, closer. They were on his bumper.

"We'll be killed!" screamed Lilac. "We'll both be killed."

"No, no," he said. "That won't happen."

He got it up to eighty, ninety, and then he passed a trooper on the interstate, and the siren came on.

In his rearview mirror, he could see that maroon-colored hooligan car flashing past the trooper, and the trooper car flashing after them.

They couldn't keep up with this car.

He got off at Masters Drive. He got off that onto another city street. He got off that street. He went a block and turned off. He got on another street, and still another. He turned several more times.

"Where are we?"

"I don't know."

"That trooper. You think he got your license plate?"

"I sure hope not."

"You were hitting ninety-five," she said. "I saw it."

"Um. I had to."

"Where are we going?"

"Way, way the hell away from that trooper."

"You think he'll follow you? How would he find you?"

"I don't know."

"You want me to hold your hand? Like this?"

Her soft, girlish fingers touched his, on the steering wheel. He got a buzz. "Want to come over to my place?"

"If you'll promise me."

"What?"

"You'll get a better place."

"I will. I promise."

"Good. Then once, but no more."

"I'll look in the paper tomorrow," he said.

She was quiet a long time. He drove straight through town and got back to his place without once getting on the interstate. He had a call when he was just getting on the outside steps.

"Go ahead," he said.

"It's not like I have the key," she said.

"Oh, that's right." He went for it in his pocket and handed it to her. He stood on the steps, going for his phone.

He saw the number. It wasn't a 911 number. It wasn't Bulge. Who, though?

"You coming in?" she asked.

"Sure."

"You don't sound so interested. Who called?"

"I don't know. I didn't answer it."

He hurried up the steps. He stood there, on the landing. Who was it anyway?

"Well, come on in. Dear god."

She stood there in front of the bed.

He came for her.

"Not so fast."

"Huh?"

"A girl doesn't go for that kind of thing. She wants to be romanced. Not attacked."

"Oh. I didn't mean—"

"Don't go all sad on me. Just don't come at me like that."

He eased toward her. He was next to her, but he wanted to kiss her hard, hard, hard.

"That's better. Do you want to get in bed with me? Is that what you want?"

"God, yes."

"It's okay since I'm pregnant. You can't alter that fact one bit. You know?"

"That's right," he said.

"Oh, I suppose you know about things like that."

"Uh, no."

"Well, you'd better."

"I will. I do. I want to marry you!"

"My god. You are a case."

"What did I do?"

"Nothing." She looked away. She put a finger to her lips. She got down on the floor and put her ear to it.

"What?"

She shushed him. "I hear something."

"What?"

"Be quiet. Listen."

He got down on the floor. He put his ear to it. He thought he heard something. Scratching noises. Then a little squeaking. Then scratching.

"Rats!" she yelled and got up.

"No, I don't think so."

"Yes—rats! Take me home! Now!"

She was up and bolting for the door.

He stopped her. "That can't be rats. Her ceiling is right below us."

"They're in the ceiling! It's awful!"

"I don't think so," he said.

But she was opening the door already, and he was behind her, out on the landing, and shutting the door, locking it, and they were on their way down to the car.

11

"Go to the police," said Bulge.

"I can't."

"And why is that?"

He tried to tell him, but it was too convoluted, and so how tell him? How he was hitting ninety—no, ninety-five—the cop siren coming on, how he didn't slow, but kept on because of those hooligans, and then in his rearview mirror how he saw those cops pulling over the hooligan car—maroon-colored, it was—but that trooper might have gotten his license number. Not that he didn't try to lose him. "If you know what I mean," said Frederick.

"You just can't stay out of trouble, can you?"

He said sure he could if hooligans like that hadn't destroyed his red car. It was absolutely destroyed. It was a real mess to look at, you bet.

"Where is it?"

Frederick got out of his chair and advanced across the room. He parted the blinds. "Down there, that red one."

Bulge moved in. He looked. "Um. Not good. Tire irons, huh?"

"Beat all to hell."

"I'd say. That seems the thing these days. Beat it with a

tire iron. Like that solves anything."

"I don't have insurance."

"You what?"

"No."

"Well, then, son, you're in a peck of trouble. You're what they call screwed."

"I know it. Have to drive that thing around like that and pay this big monthly payment. It's not fair."

"Life."

"I need a job."

"Who doesn't?"

"What?"

"It's the way of the world, kid. You have your jobs, and you have your jobs. Did you see the judge yet?"

"No."

"He was asking about you. He needs that fifteen hundred."

"I don't have fifteen hundred!"

"You owe him, son. And he's getting in a hurry. He's... well, I won't say it."

"He can't—"

"That's right, he can't. And you know, a man gets thoughts like that in his head, and that's all she wrote. He's got to have it. Follow my meaning?"

"Uh... yes."

"My best advice, get that to him before the day's out. That way... well, I don't have to spell it out surely."

"You think I can come up with fifteen hundred bucks without a job?"

"It's not a matter of what I think. You just have to. It's down to that."

"Well, I can't."

Bulge made like he was sawing a violin. "Sorry for you. Oh, so sorry." He quit. "In that case, I'd make an appearance. I'd show up within the hour and lay it all out. Say how sorry I was. Leave him some money. A flat sum of some kind. Hundred, two hundred. Good faith. Well, son, I've got to go now, plenty to do."

"Can I have that job?"

"Job? What job?"

"You said you'd let me know."

"Oh, well, sure, sure. You can file. You can start filing right this minute. Get to it now and don't play around."

"But I don't know where anything goes."

"Then how can you possibly file? Not knowing a single thing."

"I can't."

"No, not unless I teach you. But first off the judge. Here," and he pulled his billfold out, "here, here's two hundred. Two crisp one-hundred-dollar bills. That ought to do it."

"Damn. Thanks."

"Don't curse."

"Oh—okay."

"Now, then, I'll see you in an hour. Ask the judge how his day's going, hand him the two hundred, offer more, and then you're back here"—he pointed at the clock—"in an hour. Ready to work. Understand?"

"Yes, sir."

"Some lunch first. I'll send out for Chinese."

"Damn!"

"Don't curse."

"Oh—okay."

"Here, take a few more," said Bulge, and he opened his billfold again. "Here, take this."

Frederick took them. Two, three, four one-hundred-dollar bills. "Thanks!"

"And tell him I'd like a favorable ruling on my case—he'll know which. No problem there."

"Uh, but—"

"Now, then—off with you. Off, off."

"Yes, sir."

There he was at Judge Barnhart's door. It was half open, and he was wondering: Do I go in, make my appearance, my supplication?

He heard noises.

He stepped forward, and there he was, a man standing with his broad back to Frederick, reaching for a bookcase, removing a book, slamming it on top of a book parked on the desk.

And then there he was doing it again.

"Excuse me," said Frederick.

The judge turned around. Slowly. He was as round as a barrel. He looked like those English country gentlemen Frederick had seen on old movies his English teacher had shown the class. Jane Austen, that kind of thing. Or was it *Wuthering Heights*? Or something. *Great Expectations*. They all ran together in one big muddle in his mind.

"Who're you?"

"Frederick Weber, sir."

"'Frederick Weber sir.' Hmm. Well, you just step this way. You just take a chair—that one—while I take down a few books. There. That chair."

Frederick went where the judge pointed. He sat in the chair which had a nice cushion, flat but comfortable. He adjusted himself. He wanted to rest his feet on the judge's desk. It was tempting at least while the judge's back was turned, as the rotund man searched a shelf and whammed his latest selection on the growing pile. They were all thick books. Law books, it looked like. Would he have to understand any of that stuff to work in Bulge's office?

The judge came around to the large swivel chair behind his desk.

"Now, then, son, what might I do for you—besides let you off on that case—what was it? Drunk driving, petty theft, sexual assault, rape, burglary, shoplifting—what was it?"

"Assault," said Frederick, "only the man I hit—the young man, I mean—he asked for it. He called my girlfriend a—I don't want to say it."

"Bitch?"

"Yes, sir."

"Let's get it out in the open. All of it. The whole shooting match. It's best in this line of business to get everything out in the open. Shout it from the house tops!" The judge was half shouting, and someone, a woman about the judge's age, primly dressed, whom Frederick imagined was about fifty-five or so, suddenly arrived at the judge's desk. "Yes, Miriam, too loud?"

"Oh, no, your honor. No, I just need a few signatures."

"Use the stamp."

"Oh, but I can't—not on these."

"Is that right?" He extended a palm. It was a big one.

He had the papers now, and he adjusted his thick glasses and paged through one of them. He dropped them on the desk, so that they sort of sailed down there. He then grabbed a large pen and flipped through those pages and worked with that pen, with obvious effort.

They were soon back in the woman's hands. "Thank you, your honor." She had a bright smile, with large blue eyes. Her lips were colored bright red, and Frederick caught a smudge in the corner of one lip. That was her right one. His left, her right. He couldn't help but stare.

"No more today, though," said the judge, raising his glasses. "Save them for tomorrow—all righty?"

"Yes, your honor."

"Oh, stop calling me that."

"Yes, sir."

"Doug," he said. "Please."

"But I really, I really—"

"Doug!"

"Yes, sir."

"Jeez! Are you deaf? Doug!"

"Yes, Doug."

"Good. Go to lunch or something."

"It's only ten-thirty," she said. "I'm not hungry either."

"Lie down then on that couch I bought you."

"Okay... Doug."

"Alrighty."

Frederick wanted to put his feet up. He really wanted to put his feet up on the judge's desk. It would be so comfortable.

"Assault," said the judge.

"Yes, sir."

"Your honor."

"Yes, your honor."

"Assault."

"Horatio Dark."

"That scum? Mobster kid. Why'd you stop with assault? What was in your head, son, or your fists? Mobsters like that need to be dealt with. You think we have a chance with the law? Hell fire, not a snowball's chance. Oh, they always squeak through. They find ways. Get them on tax evasion—there's your best bet. Works every time. You think a scum like that pays his taxes? You think he'd know the IRS from a hole in the ground? No, son, I just wish. But if horses were wishes. Huh? Jeez!"

Frederick didn't want to say it, but something compelled him to. "I was happy, really happy, that you... you let me off, your honor, sir."

A large fist came down on the desk.

Frederick fell back.

"Let you off! No judge worth his salt lets a man off. I don't appreciate the slanderous remark you just made, son."

"Oh, I didn't mean to—"

"Where's my money?"

"What?"

"Clean your ears out. Where's my money?"

Frederick went for his billfold. He drew out the bills, the hundreds. And then he laid the small pile, six of them, with ends curling up, on the judge's shiny desk. He patted them down so they were halfway orderly.

"Well, now." The judge began to count them. Silently. Then he nodded. Then he turned toward Frederick with a scowl. "Please shut that door, son."

"Yes, your honor." Frederick went for it.

"This is not even half. You think I can swing a deal... or get what I want, what I've been... counting on... for several days now... for this?"

"That's all I have, your honor."

"Well, it's too bad. Don't you have a job?"

"I'm in high school, sir."

"Your honor."

"Yes, sir. Your honor."

"Well... it's a start, but let's see a little more coming in... soon. Now, then, where did you get this money?"

"From Mr. Bulge, sir—your honor."

"For what?"

"For... working for him. I have a job, sir. Your honor."

"You find it so difficult to say 'Your Honor,' don't you? You work for Mr. Bulge, attorney-at-law?"

"Yes—your honor."

"When did that begin?"

"Today, sir. Your honor."

"Today. Then you didn't earn it. Was it an advance?"

"Yes, sir. I mean 'your honor.'"

"Six-hundred-dollar advance. Did he say anything about all this? Did he spout anything out that I should know about?"

"Well, your honor, he said he hoped you'd provide a good judgment for a case—"

"A bribe! I knew it!"

"Oh, no, your honor."

"Well, as bribes go, it comes up short, now doesn't it? I'm left wondering. I'm left wondering... when the next nine hundred will appear... right on my desk here."

"I'll have it soon, sir."

"By god, son, I won't tell you again: It's 'Your Honor!'"

"Yes, sir. Your honor."

"Bring me the nine hundred in an hour or two."

"An hour... where would I get that?"

"Get, get. How would I know? Get that nine hundred, or you know what they say about grass."

"Yes, your honor."

"Carry on, now, son." He gave him a little salute.

12

Out in his red car, smashed up, with dents and crashed-in front windows, Frederick took off.

He was a few blocks down a major thoroughfare when he spotted a police cruiser cornering from a side street, and the siren blew.

No place to pull over. The siren ramping up, a wailing shriek.

He pulled to a stop on the street. Blocking traffic. In his rearview mirror, he could see the cruiser advancing, the driver's door opening, the cop stepping out.

He went for his billfold. He went for the papers on the car.

The cop was suddenly at his window. With mirrored sunglasses. "Get in a wreck or something? This window here is about to fall out. The same for the other. License and registration, please."

Those mirrored sunglasses disturbed Frederick. He felt his legs grow weak. His hand grew shaky.

He delivered the papers on the car with his driver's license on top. It meant going over the top of the smashed-in window.

"Watch out, sir," said the cop. And then he sized things

up. "A very expensive car, it looks like. In very bad shape, isn't it? I'm assuming you're on your way to a body shop."

"I've been there, sir—officer."

"What's that mean?" He scrutinized the license, then handed it back.

"I was there, and I got kind of an estimate."

"What do you mean 'kind of'?"

"Well, other damages soon followed. For instance, this and that window," he said, pointing to his driver's-side window and then the passenger front window, both crushed and cracked in.

"Did you report the accident, sir?"

"It wasn't an accident, officer. It was on purpose."

"Pardon? What's that mean?"

"A guy, a hooligan, took a tire iron to it. Another took another. Hooligans. That's what they were."

"Did you report it?"

"Not yet."

"Why not?"

"Well."

"You've got to do this if you want your damages fixed. And judging by the look of it, there are a lot of damages. As long as it wasn't a moving violation, it's up to you— except for this window—and the other one. I'm going to impound this vehicle until it's fixed."

"Oh, no, officer. Please..."

"Please exit the car at this time," said the cop.

"Yes, sir. Officer."

He stepped out of the car.

The cop stood there, looking down at him with those mirrored glasses. He was six feet plus.

"What... what do I do next?" said Frederick.

"If you need a ride, sir, I'll give you one to your destination—as long as it's inside the city limits."

"I'll be okay," said Frederick. He was hugely bothered by those mirror sunglasses. He moved off a few feet, and then he wondered if he'd done something wrong.

"It's entirely up to you. You'll find your impounded car at this address." He handed Frederick a card.

※ ※ ※

Frederick took to the sidewalk. It was another twenty minutes when he saw the sign:

PAYDAY LOANS:
GET YOUR CASH NOW!
FAST DELIVERY!

He entered.

There, settled in a row of chairs, were a dozen or more people. One had a long white beard. He had his face in his hands. A woman was settled back, looking asleep. A young man about his age, or a little older, was yawning.

He stood looking out the plate glass window. Then he saw it: a huge tow truck with his bashed-in red sports car up there being carried off. He started to cry out, but the young man yawned again, and he shut up.

And then he realized he didn't have his cell phone.

A pretty young woman with blue eyes was eyeing them all. "Who's next?"

The young guy, about his age, stepped forward. "Me, ma'am."

"Don't call me 'ma'am.' Please. If you would, please refrain from doing so."

"Oh, sorry."

"An associate will now see you." She pointed back to the rows of desks. "The man in the blue shirt."

"Thank you."

Frederick approached the counter.

"You'll have to wait, sir."

"I just have a question. Do you know where this place is?" He handed her the card. He pointed at the window. "I just saw—"

She gave him a look. "Umm, yes. About five miles to the south. Get on the interstate, go about three miles—"

"I'll be taking a cab."

"Cab?"

"My car. It's not so good."

"Motor problems?"

"No—the body."

"Umm. What about the body?"

"Caved in hood, windows broken."

"My god. But please have a seat."

He did. For an hour.

And then the woman motioned at him with a twinkling eye. "Your time has come. See that man in the red shirt?"

"Yes, ma'am."

"Ma'am?"

"No... I mean..."

She shook her head. A smile crept over those supple red lips. "I do hope your body—well, I mean, you know what I mean."

"Yes, I do. Thanks."

"Oh, it's nothing."

God, she was beautiful. He thought thoughts he was ashamed to think, because what if Lilac could read his various thoughts? But he couldn't seem to help himself. He glanced back at her as he was making his way back to the man in the red shirt. She smiled. It was such a nice smile. Such lovely dimples. Such curvaceous curves. He waved.

The man in the red shirt signaled the chair at his desk.

Frederick took it.

"Now, then," said the man in the red shirt, "just what can I do for you? I assume I can do something for you, or otherwise you wouldn't be here. You'd be out zooming up and down the highways and byways after some girly, or you'd be at some hotspot bar with your buds, raising a few, or you'd be sticking your nose in a book, which wouldn't be me, but... it takes all kinds, now doesn't it?"

"Yes, sir."

"Oh, don't call me 'sir'—I can't be much older than you. What're you, eighteen, nineteen, twenty?"

"Seventeen."

"Um. Don't think we can make a loan to you, then. You've got to be at least eighteen."

"I turn eighteen soon."

"Too bad, so sad."

"I bought a car."

"Pardon? You what?"

"Yes—I did."

"Well, those guys probably ignored or lied about your age. They'll sell a car to a muskrat. Get them off the lot, get a guy, or girl, driving it, that's their thing. You know?"

"So... if I did that, I could surely get a little cash."

"How much is a 'little'?"

"Fifteen hundred. Or better yet, two thousand."

"Ooh, that's more than a little. Now if you were saying three hundred, say, well, we might be able to do some business as long as I fudged a thing or two. Of course we don't loan that little. We don't loan anything less than a thousand."

"Then why—"

"But your age. Too bad."

"But if only—"

"Shhh. Two thousand?"

"Fifteen hundred at least."

"Better make it two thousand if we're talking anything because if you're in for a penny, you know? Got it?"

"Sure." He settled back in the red plastic chair.

"Okay, then. Just a note or two to get us started. What

do you need this money for?"   A big white tooth crept over the man's lumpy lower lips.

"Uh, well, you see, there's this judge. I guess, just to be honest—"

"No, I don't want to hear it. Just give me something I can put on this pad here. To store in my computer here."

It was a yellow legal pad. It was a sleek looking computer. Gray. Frederick couldn't see what he'd already written. He had written it in cursive, and it was slanting way to the right, or was that the left? He couldn't decide since it was upside down from where he was looking at it.

Suddenly, that delicious looking young girl from the counter was showing up with a cup of coffee. "Thought you might like this," she said. She was leaning over exposing her cleavage. It was like nothing he'd ever seen.

"Umm," he said. "Yes."

"Just thought you would," she said, and winked.

He started to say something but decided it had better wait since she was already heading back to her station at the counter. And he was watching her, his insides fluttering, as she regained that post.

"What a hottie, huh?"

He flinched. "Uh, yes."

"Ginger's her name. Nice name. Ginger Fling—if you want the whole dope." He grinned. He laid a hand on Frederick's shoulder. "She must have taken to you, bringing that cup of coffee there. You want cream?"

"Sure."

The man in the red shirt handed him a package.

"You want a woman? She's for you."

"I've got a woman," said Frederick.

"Maybe two, then," said the man in the red shirt.

"No, no."

"Now, then, all that aside. What's with this two thousand you need? What's so important? Down on a car? Big computer? Gambling debts?"

"No, no. Like I said, this judge..."

"I don't want to hear it. I hate it when guys like you are fined, sent to jail till you can pay the stinking fine. I've had it up to my ears with all that. Hell, what choice do you have?"

"None."

"Okay, we'll work around the age thing..." He placed a finger to his lips and said, "Let me see your driver's license."

Frederick went for it.

"Hmm. We'll just change that August 21 to March 21. Anybody can make a mistake, can't they? A young man comes in, he wants to get a good start on life—right? And there he is, having just turned eighteen, and the world's his oyster. Right?"

"Yes, sir. I suppose—yes. Mr.—"

"No, no, if you're going to call me anything, call me Duane. Not Mr. Colfax."

Frederick suddenly noticed the name plate in front of him on the desk. He hadn't seen it before.

"Okay, Duane."

"That's better. Makes me feel old if somebody calls me 'Mr. Colfax'. I'm only twenty-nine, and who wants that?"

"No."

"Two thousand. Okay, done. Now, then, the interest is going to be... well, a bit startling. To say the least."

"How much?"

"Ha! You ask. Seven hundred percent. If you keep it out a year, and you borrow two thousand, you owe roughly thirteen thousand dollars. A real bite in the butt, ain't it now?"

"Uh, isn't that fourteen thousand—"

"Oh, right. Honest type, huh?"

"I can't pay that!"

"No one can, unless they're rich and they wouldn't be here in the first place if they were. You're looking at a payment of... let's see, a little over seven hundred a month. Give or take."

"I can't do it."

The man in the red shirt leaned over. "No one can. Take bankruptcy or something. They'll hunt you down wherever you go; they'll collect one way or the other if you don't. But forget all that," he said and grinned, whispering even more softly, "this is an illegal loan. They won't collect a thing on this one. Not legally they won't!"

"Oh."

"But they have other ways. Or need I mention those?"

"No."

"But legally... well, just an honest mistake on my part."

"Um. You get fired?"

"Fired? Who wants the job anyway?"

"I guess, then... heck..."

"You might make the first payment, just to show good faith."

"Okay."

❧ ❧ ❧

On the way out, he accosted Ginger. "Would you... would you like to go out?"

"In that wreck of yours?"

"Well."

"If you'll wait a few hours, I'll give you a ride out there—to that place where they've pastured your car."

"Oh, thanks."

"Have a seat over there," she said, and smiled.

13

They flew over the interstate together in her hot little jeep. Once she placed a hand on his knee and smiled. She made turns, more turns, still more turns and then she pulled into a large lot packed with a hundred or more cars.

"Um," she said. "This always gets me." And she went down one long row. "Like airport parking. Tell me if you see it."

He looked. He didn't.

More rows. More. Still more.

He looked. He didn't.

And then he did. That red beauty, only it wasn't a beauty—not anymore, it wasn't. Wrecked, ruined, that's what it was.

"There," he said.

She pulled up. She stopped.

He got out of the car. She got out. "Say, that does have body problems. It's a real mess."

"Locked. It's locked," he said.

"Of course it's locked. But with that broken window, what difference could it make? Let's go check."

She got back in her car. He did too.

She drove around and then up to a long, flat building. "In there," she said. "You follow me. Just follow me."

"Do you know... you know?"

"Happened to my boyfriend at least five times. Or was it six?"

"Your boyfriend?"

"Gone. Done with."

"Oh."

"Not dead, but close to it."

"Um."

"Come on."

He followed her, hyped up on her wiggly hips, which that car coat she sported didn't hide. He tried not to look. They came to the building, and she opened the door for him. He stepped in.

"Your driver's license, please, sir," said an official. He had a white shirt on. No tie, though.

Frederick presented it.

"Well, now."

"What?"

"Well, now."

"What!"

"Well." He was viewing his computer. "That'll be one thousand for the towing. Five hundred for the release fee."

"Huh? What?"

"Yes. Yes," said the official. He had a long chin and pointed nose.

Ginger moved forward. She laid her pretty fingers on the counter. "Is this some kind of scam?"

"No, ma'am, those are the costs to have that automobile released and to pay the towing that got it here."

Frederick went for his billfold. All he had was the check made out to him by the payday loans place. He presented it.

"Third party check—we don't take them," said the official. He pointed behind him.

Frederick looked up. A sign: No Third Party Checks.

"I can vouch for it," said Ginger. "He just borrowed it, and I'm an employee there."

"No third party checks, ma'am."

"You keep that up, and I'll smack you," she said.

"What? Keep what up?"

"Calling me ma'am'—that's what."

"Just trying to be civil, 'ma'am."

She raised a hand, and then moved forward. In the man's face. "Then call this number." She handed him a card.

He glanced at it. "Why would I do that?"

"Because it's a legitimate place and they made a legitimate loan. That's why."

"It makes no difference. No third party checks."

"Well, damn, what the—"

"How late are you open?" asked Frederick.

"Till ten, and you won't find many impoundment lots open till ten—no sir."

"Bully," she said.

"Policy," he said.

"You're just so customer friendly, aren't you?" she said on the way out.

"There's one place open that'll cash that check for you —just one. But it'll cost you."

"How much?"

"We'll see when we get there."

❦ ❦ ❦

It was HARRY'S PAWN SHOP.

"Five hundred," he said. He looked grizzled. He coated his chapped lips with a tentative tongue. "And that's taking a risk."

"Why?"

"Who knows with that place? How long it'll last."

"Well, I hope it does. My job," she said.

"Well, it just might fold, little lady. Anytime."

"No—to your five hundred," she said.

"Four hundred."

"No to that."

"Three hundred."

"No."

"Two."

"No. Let's go," she said. "You can take it to the bank first thing tomorrow."

"One," said the pawn broker.

"No!"

"Fifty!"

"No, damn it. Get reasonable, and we've got a deal."

"Twenty."

She looked at Frederick, then whispered in his ear.

"Ten," she said, "and you've got a deal."

"Ten, fine, fine." He took the check and wrote on it, then started peeling off hundreds from a roll. They were old hundreds. Worn. Not crispy. Where had they all been?

"Thanks, I suppose," said Ginger.

"Better not bounce," said the pawn broker.

❦ ❦ ❦

Back in the car, she raised a finger. "Towing's going to be bad, so you don't want to get your average tow truck.

We'll get my boyfriend—my ex."

She got on the interstate, and in a mile or so, got off. She headed through city streets, old city streets, lined with tall trees, snow against curbs, sagging porches. Sagging roofs. The houses looked worse and worse. Dilapidated.

"He's a druggie, but basically a good guy. Just don't get on his bad side. That's my recommendation."

"How... how would I do that?"

"Oh, you'll know. He'll get this look, like a dog baring its teeth. You know?"

"Uh..."

"He actually does bare his teeth. And they're sharp."

"Oh."

"Yes."

It was getting dark now. The moon was hanging over the streets, over the dark, snow-covered trees. The light was like yellow water.

She pulled into the driveway of a shotgun house with a Confederate flag in the front yard. She sat there for a moment. "Just watch what you say. It depends on what he's high on. Some highs are good, some not so good."

"Um," he said.

She got out of the car. He did too.

She made her way up the rickety porch to the door and knocked. She knocked three, four times. "Damn. Show up, will you?"

The door came open. There he stood. A scraggly beard. Wild hair, every which way.

"Hey, darlin," he said, grabbing her. "How's tricks?"

"Take your hands off me." She pulled loose.

"This your new man?"

"Just a friend. He needs a tow." She said where, how much, and would he give him some sort of a break—for her?

"Why would I do that?"

"For me."

"How about for me?"

"We'll see," she said, and gave Frederick a look.

"How about five hundred?"

"No! And don't play games. One hundred, and that's it. You can buy some weed for that, and that's all you're getting."

"Well, maybe I don't like that."

"Well, maybe that's all you're getting, like I said."

"Have to be tomorrow."

"No! It has to be tonight. Right this minute."

"What? Naw!"

"It's the impoundment lot. You know where that is. Now don't you? But you've got just an hour to get out there—before they close."

"Sure, sure."

"We'll meet you out there. And don't you fail to show. Or you'll be sorry. You know?"

"Yeah," he said. "I reckon." He gave her an ugly leer.

She turned and went. "One of these days he'll be jailed for good," she said.

❧ ❧ ❧

Out at the impoundment lot, they waited fifteen minutes.

"Where is he?" said Ginger, biting a nail. "I'll bet he doesn't show. If I know him, he'll have to smoke one, and then he'll leave. And he'll be late, too late, and they'll have already closed."

"No car," said Frederick. "I don't have a car."

"Now, now." She laid a hand on his knee.

He got a buzz.

"I've got to have that car, you know."

"That car's going to cost you a bunch of money to fix. How'd that happen?"

"Hooligans."

"Huh? Who? Where?"

He described the lot in front of the Bronco Motel and Steakhouse. And where that was.

"What were you doing there? You have a girl with you?"

"Uh, yeah... just to get something to eat."

"I'm sure."

Suddenly he spotted the tow truck. It was an ugly black thing lunging and lunging, screeching and squalling. Ginger got out and flagged her ex down. When he'd pulled up, she said to Frederick, "Now go on in and pay that whopping fee and we'll meet you out here."

※ ※ ※

He did. All that cash. Wiped out. What to do?

There his red car was meanwhile being hooked up to that black tow truck. And then that was done, and they were on their way, following her druggie ex out to the body shop.

"You'll get an estimate probably in a few days," she said. "And I can't imagine what it'll be. You might as well trade it in for a new one. It's totaled is what I think."

"I can't do that."

"That's so sad," she said and again placed her hand on his knee.

He started toward her, but thought better of it.

※ ※ ※

They were headed back now. He told her to drop him off in front of his lawyer's office.

"This late?"

"I have to meet him."

"At this hour?"

"If he's still there." He had his cell phone back now, and he tried the number.

"Mr. Weber. Did you see him?"

"Yes—but I need... more money," he whispered.

"Can't hear you."

He whispered it again.

"Still can't hear you."

"Are you there—in your office?"

"Sure. Always am. This is where you'll find me, twenty-four seven."

"Really?"

"Call me when you get here and I'll ring you in."

He turned to Ginger. "Take a right here."

❧ ❧ ❧

She bid him goodbye with a wave and a kiss and said, "You know where to find me."

"I'll be there soon enough," he said. "I need another loan, it looks like."

"Oh, well, next time I'll handle your loan, sweetie."

Sweetie?

"Bye," he said. "Bye."

"Bye now," she said.

14

He got rung in, and he was soon in Mr. Bulge's office.

"What'd he say?"

"Six hundred wasn't enough. He wants the whole fifteen."

"Well, now, if the judge says fifteen hundred, you can bet this is exactly what he means. What he wants. You see he's got demands he's got to meet, and if he can't meet those demands, he's in a bad way."

"Yeah, but—"

"You've got to understand his needs, not just yours."

Sure, he said, he did, and he'd even borrowed two thousand from one of those payday loan places, but then he had to pay to get his car out of the impoundment lot and that took almost every dollar he had, and now he was going to have to borrow even more from that payday place —if he could.

"Ooh, son, never borrow from a payday place. They're run by the mob. They don't get their money back on a timely basis? They break bones. Go to the bank. That's your best bet, always."

"I have no collateral. I have no job."

"Them's the breaks. Now, sir, what about doing that

filing and so forth for me? Taking out the trash."

"I had a hard day."

"Who hasn't?"

"I'm considerably bad off."

"Take a rest then, on that couch."

Mr. Bulge pointed.

He went to it and lay down. It made a whooshing noise. How comfortable it was.

He awoke confused. He was being shaken.

"Mr. Weber."

"Yes?"

"The judge—you should contact him soon. I'm sure he's in his chambers waiting."

"He doesn't go home?"

"Sometimes. But not when he's got a big fish on the line. You know, that lovely little fishie?"

"They won't... in there, will they?"

"No, no. No, they'll go to some out-of-the-way place, one of those down-and-out motels that look like somebody ought to take a match to them—probably fifty to a hundred miles away—to hide their faces, you see."

"What'll I do? What do you propose I do?"

"I'm a lawyer, not a therapist."

"I'm sick, sick, sick of everything!"

"Now, now," said Mr. Bulge. "Now, now." He laid a fatherly hand on Frederick's shoulder.

"What can I do? Do?"

Bulge came forth with his billfold. "What you do is give him a little more, just to show good faith." He drew out some bills and handed them to Frederick. Then he came forth with a pocketful of loose change.

Frederick counted it all: three twenties and one dollar and eighty-one cents in change.

"But he wants fifteen hundred."

"Sure. But we don't always get what we want, now do we? You take that to the man, you apologize, and maybe he'll let you off. Maybe he sure will."

"Really?"

"But maybe he won't."

"Um!"

"Where you made your big mistake, son, is springing that car from the impoundment lot. You would've had your fifteen hundred, but see, you thought better of getting that car in your hands. Isn't that right?"

"Yes, sir."

"Now, go over there, see the judge, and beg forgiveness."

"I don't know... I'm not sure I can."

"Down on your knees. You want to practice? That's okay. That's understood. I could give pointers."

"I don't know. I don't. I just—just sixty dollars?"

"You want me to come with you? Is that what you want?"

"Would you?"

"No, son. I'm busy, and you should be helping me out instead of doing what you're doing, but I guess I can't get good help, now can I? Go, go. Be gone with you."

🌿 🌿 🌿

He was outside the judge's door, and it was past eleven. He tried to hear inside if there was anything going on, but he couldn't make out anything.

And then there was the noise of furniture moving. Was that a desk? A bookcase? It wasn't a chair, was it? No, a chair wouldn't make that kind of noise. Loud, boisterous. Making room for...?

Finally, he knocked. But just lightly.

Nothing. So he knocked again.

Nothing.

And so he knocked still another time.

He knocked still again. Harder this time. In fact, he pounded on the door.

Now he heard footsteps. Yes, those were distinctly footsteps.

The door screeched open. A very loud screech. Un-oiled hinges? It was a very big door. It shone like it had been polished. The judge stood there, his shirt loose, his tie loose, a goofy look on his face, and behind him, Frederick caught a fleshy looking woman. In her underwear. That was all. Pink. Prancing about.

"I'm sorry, your honor. I'm sorry. Here, here I've brought you something. He had it in his right-hand pocket for easy delivery. He went for it. He grabbed it all up, those three twenties, wadded up, sort of, plus the dollar and eighty-one cents in loose change. Quarters, he saw, dimes he saw, copper pennies. A veritable smorgasbord of loose change. He went for the judge's palm, dumped it all there, and backed away, just slightly.

"Why thank you, son. Why thank you."

The judge half closed the door, but it was open enough that Frederick saw the woman's bare bosom. He felt faint. He leaned against the wall.

"You needing something, son? You don't look so good."

The judge was stepping out now, closing the door behind him. He worked at his loosened tie. "Anything I can do, son?"

"I don't have fifteen hundred, sir."

"Your honor."

"Your honor."

The judge put his ear up to the door. He turned back to Frederick. "Then get it. Get it soon."

Frederick watched as the judge turned the door knob, a shiny one, stepped in, and the door screeched closed.

Inside, there were noises.

He placed his ear up against the door.

# 15

Back at Bulge's he spent until three in the morning filing, dusting, sweeping, and taking breaks lying on the couch, sleeping.

"Time you left," said Bulge.

"I need an advance. To get my car fixed."

"What you need is the prosecuting attorney to nab those hooligans. Be sure to go double: criminal plus civil charges. And be sure you emphasize emotional pain. Juries understand emotional pain. Every one of us understands that. Now don't we?"

"Yes, I do miss that car. Plenty."

"Sure you do. Sure you do. Be sure to testify in court. Lay it on thick. Cry a lot. Sob. Leak tears! Juries will eat that up, especially the women jurors."

"Cry?"

"Oh, yes, a lot."

He decided not to pursue this. Instead, he said, "Where do I start? What do I do?"

"Don't fix that car. Leave it as it is. You want those jurors watching a slide show. Or rather a video. Make it long. No, short. But not too short. And maybe they'll even be ushered over to look out the window at it, all beaten up, if we can reserve a space that morning."

"Which morning?"

"The morning of the trial. Dress up. Sure, your hooligans will dress up too, but you make sure you're dressed to the nines. A poor sap with his car wrecked, beaten to death by those defendants, those hooligans. That'll play well. You bet."

"It's true."

"Did I say it wasn't?"

"No, sir."

"Well, then, let's get on with it. Vandalism in the first degree."

"What do I do?"

"We'll sic the prostituting attorney on them. Haven't you been listening?"

"Yes, but I don't know their names or where they live, or—"

"Then how do you expect the DA to do his job?"

"I tried to find out, but they did further damage to my vehicle."

"You sound like a claims adjustor. Be less formal, please."

"Yes, sir."

"Now, then, what do you think their names are? Spill them, son."

"How would I know?"

"We'll let this up to the cops. We'll make sure they do their job."

"I couldn't go to the cops."

"What? Why not?"

He explained, as before. About hitting ninety—no, ninety-five—trying to escape from those hooligans, the trooper car after him, and then they stopped the hooligans. But maybe they got his plate number. He was afraid to contact them.

"Well, now, we'll just see what your lawyer can swing."

It was Bulge's considered opinion that he should go after those hooligans, only this time with some force. One didn't do a thing like this alone. One got a hitman or a ruffian with some creds, a rap sheet, like a resume for an interview, proof that he could do the job. In other words, said Bulge, you interview him. You know, who, what, when, where, and why.

"Who do I get?"

"It's whom."

"What?"

"Whom instead of who."

"Oh."

"Horatio Dark. There's your man."

"But I popped him just once and nearly put him in his grave."

"Lucky punch. A mobster goes down too, you know. You know what they say about the bigger they are."

"Yeah."

"There's your ticket, son. Mr. Dark."

"His father?"

"No, no. Horatio, the young stud you decked."

"Oh."

"Now, then I'll be calling the cops, so you skedaddle."

"Yes, sir."

"And don't call me 'sir.'"

"No?"

"Call me Mr. Bulge."

"Yes, sir. Mr. Bulge."

"Thank you."

✺ ✺ ✺

Now he was on his way to the Dark residence. On foot, of course. His car was at that body shop to get an estimate. He'd have to walk out there later after he'd had several cups of coffee. But right now he must get hold of Horatio Dark because how was he supposed to get it fixed if he didn't track down those hooligans?

✺ ✺ ✺

He came to a house that looked almost identical to Lilac Johnson's house, with a tree in the exact same place where her tree was, a red front door, a bedroom window looking out on the front lawn, with an identical lamp lighted, and cranberry-colored curtains open. This wasn't the Johnson place; it looked like it, but it wasn't.

It was almost five in the morning. Dark now, but soon the sun would rise. He knocked lightly on the door.

He stood there for a few moments, and then he knocked again.

Nothing stirring.

Suddenly a squeak, and a man appeared. "Yes? Who are you? Is there an emergency? Is my son hurt again? Are you a cop?"

"No, sir. I was looking for your son. Horatio, that is."

"Him? You won't find him here. He has a place close to the school. He's in school, you know, repeating for the third time his senior year. If you know him at all, you know that. But at least he's out of the hospital. That dreadful mother—well, my language is getting ahead of me. That dreadful son—there I did it again. That miserable wretch, I should say, who punched my son's lights out that way—a sucker punch, it was. Cold-cocked him, he did. That nearly broke my heart to see him at death's door. Well, he's all right now, but there for a while—who are you exactly? A friend? A foe? Who are you?"

Frederick said it without delay, without temporizing.

"Him? You're him?"

"Yes, sir."

"Might you come in, then, young man?"

"Uh... but I'm wanting to see your son, and you say he's not here."

"Do you doubt me?"

"No, sir."

"Then come on in. Want a whiskey? A bit of bourbon?"

"I'm not of age."

"So?"

"At this hour?"

"Oh, I don't pay attention to that at all. Whatever hour we're looking at is good for whiskey or wine. I'm not particularly picky. One's as good as the other, though I must say I prefer whiskey as long as it's bourbon. No Scotch. I hate Scotch. Bourbon. It must be with a cola. Or water—water's all right. So medicinal tasting. Reminds me of that bad stuff my doctor gave me once when I had terrible chest congestion, wheezing painfully like I'd been shot. Well. Sure. Here," he said, guiding Frederick through one room, then into another, then into still another, "Let us have a convivial drink together. What do you say, sir?"

He guided Frederick to a leather chair and gave him a little push. Frederick landed in it, and the cushions let out a whoosh of air. He had to adjust himself, to sit forward a little, and then back. He suddenly felt extremely comfortable. But uncomfortable, too. His stomach was doing strange things. Something not right was rising in his throat.

"Smoke?"

"No, sir."

"No need to call me 'sir,' sir—just call me Mr. Dark."

"Yes, sir. I mean Mr. Dark."

"That's better. Now, you see, I've got a bone to pick with you. I'll bet you know what it is too."

"Yes, sir. Punching out your son."

"Oh, heavens no. No! He deserved it. I'm sure. No, it's not that at all."

"What then?"

"I'm fixing drinks right now, son, so I'll have to delay my answer. You know, my wife left me shortly after you showed up. In that hospital room, I mean. She said, 'Harry, you will either go after that little twerp, or I'll leave you.' That's what she said—her exact words. But did I come after this man? No. I let him go. I let him get away with what was almost murder. Ha!"

"Uh, why are you laughing, sir—er, Mr. Dark?"

"Life is funny, isn't it? Now, here are our two drinks. My fourth since about midnight. I've been cutting down, you see. First I was increasing, then I've been cutting down."

"Good."

"You think so?"

"Yes. That's good."

"You're a moderate drinker, I assume."

"Mostly."

"When you hit my son, were you drunk?"

"Oh, no, sir—well, a little. Yes, to be honest, a little."

"Then we can blame your dastardly deed on the devil's brew, can't we?"

"Yes, but you see, it was when he said that about my girlfriend—"

"I've heard the tale. Heard it enough. Yada yada. More yada. Don't bother me with it. He deserved it, richly deserved it, but... we're a proud family, son, and that's why my wife was so insistent on my hunting down the culprit—namely you. She's a very exacting woman, you see."

Mr. Dark handed him a drink. It was in a short, fat glass.

He took a sniff of it, then a taste. Just a taste.

"Think I'm about to poison you, son?"

"No, sir. Mr. Dark."

"I don't operate in that manner, son."

A gray morning light was making its way between the parted curtains, and there was something wrong with it. It seemed sick somehow. There was a dull yellow in it wanting to burst through. Watery. He couldn't explain it. He couldn't say what it was.

"If he hadn't—"

"We know, we know. A good point, I'm sure. Now, I'll tell you a little story, son. Do you want to hear a story? A little story?"

"Yes, sir."

"Call me Mr. Dark."

"Mr. Dark."

"You'll get used to it. We can get used to practically anything, even pain. Except for some kinds of pain. Some kinds you never get used to. Do you follow my meaning?"

He sat forward. "Yes, sir. Mr. Dark."

"Good. For instance, no one at the stake ever got used to the fire at their feet. Wouldn't you agree?"

"Uh. Yes."

"Mr. Dark."

"Mr. Dark."

"No, there would be no possibility—even the remotest possibility that anyone, you, me, or John Q. Citizen could ever get used to such a thing. Could they?"

"No."

"Mr. Dark."

"Mr. Dark."

"No they wouldn't. They couldn't. They wouldn't get used to certain emotional or psychological pains either. For instance, the loss of a loved one. The loss of a dear loved one. The death of a beautiful woman. Do you follow?"

"Yes."

"Read your Poe."

"Oh, yes. I did—"

"You follow me, then."

"Yes, sir. Mr. Dark."

"Good. Because, you see, I have arranged for a bit of... well, I'm not going to say payback. But perhaps it is that since it has to do with settling the score. Right now, you see, there is a problem with one score being above the other, party to party. One party's score is much above the other's. This seems unfair and problematic. Are you familiar with the social contract?"

"Uh, no."

"Well, in my line of business, there must be an equaling, you see. Such equalizing—and reconciliations— is arranged in what we call sit-downs."

"What... what are you referring to?"

"What indeed am I referring to?"

Mr. Dark, a big man, broad shoulders, bull neck, was blocking half the doorway, at least half of it, and Frederick was feeling that the man was not going to allow him to get through the two other rooms he must pass through to get to the front door.

"I'm sorry about... what happened."

"Yes, sir. As you should be. As you certainly should be. But let's move beyond that. Let's decide on what would even the score—just a little at least."

"I don't know. I don't have a lot of money."

"Oh, money!"

"That's not it?"

"Hardly. I have plenty of money, son. I don't need more. My wife left me, and some other man's taking care of her, buying her everything she needs and wants—and believe me, that's a considerable lot. A tremendous lot. So she's not a drain anymore. No, money is not the object here."

"But equaling..."

"Yes, sir, that's right."

"What do you mean... by that?" He was on his way to the doorway. He was on his way to Mr. Dark's physical body blocking that doorway.

"What do I mean? What could I possibly mean?"

Now he was straight in front of Mr. Dark. The man shook his head. A little grin, a nasty one, with dog-looking incisors, was working on his lips.

"Would you, Mr. Dark, allow me to pass?"

The man shook his head.

"Please?"

The man shook his head. And then he drew out a pistol, large, bright silver. Shiny. He held it up. He didn't point it, but he held it up, letting it rest against his chest, pointed toward his chin. And then he moved it so that it was at an angle. And then, so that it was pointed directly at Frederick. "Bang," he said.

"Please," said Frederick.

"Bang, bang."

"I really didn't mean to. To do it. I know you're... connected, but I didn't do anything... mean to do anything that would upset... a mobster. I know you've got your protocols, and I understand, but it's not like I borrowed money at some ruinous rate... well, I did but not from some mobster... or I hope it wasn't, being one of those payday loan places, you know, so anyway, I didn't mean it that way... really."

"Mobster?"

"Aren't you?"

"Naw. Not me. Now my son, that's a different deal. He's one through and through. You probably heard that, didn't you?"

"Yes... Mr. Dark."

"Well, don't believe everything you hear, but in this case believe it. He's a man who doesn't forget either. No, he's like an elephant in that way."

"Elephant."

"But he's not afraid of mice, sir."

"Well, I wanted to find him because I had a job for him to do, if he would do it."

"Is that so? And what job is that?"

"Hooligans," said Frederick. "Hooligans have ruined my car—my red sports car."

"Hooligans."

"That's right."

"Who are these hooligans? Where are these hooligans?"

He asked for paper. Mr. Dark went to a desk across the room. Frederick could escape right now, but he didn't want to. He was intending to draw a map, such as it was.

"Here," said Mr. Dark. "Come this way." He held up a pen.

Frederick advanced toward the desk. He trembled, just slightly. This would be like a Geography assignment, sketching out a map, only in this case not of a country or of countries.

Mr. Dark held the gun at an angle away from Frederick. He had a look on his face.

Frederick took the pen and drew a simple map. He drew a line for the interstate. He made a mark where the first motel and steakhouse was. He wrote Cock & Bull. He made a mark where the second one was. He wrote Bronco. He made a mark where the third was. He wrote The Last Roundup. He held up the piece of paper. He said, "It's the second one, that Bronco place."

"Well, now," said Mr. Dark. "That's where the hooligans are, is that it?"

"Yes, Mr. Dark. The Bronco."

"Ah! It's seems to me, son, that a simple tool in my possession would rectify this situation. This little matter.

The baseball bat has certain properties... well, let us say that it's a mobster's first choice. Am I making sense here? Am I?"

"Yes, sir. Yes, Mr. Dark."

"Then we have it, do we not?"

"Yes, sir."

And then Mr. Dark poked him hard in the solar plexus with his index finger. "We'll settle up later, you and me."

He let out a groan. "Yes, Mr. Dark."

"Take a nap first, son."

"Huh?"

"Nap."

❧ ❧ ❧

But he couldn't, even on the couch where Mr. Dark tucked him in with the blanket. Not even with the pillow, which Mr. Dark slid under his head.

He lay there awake, worried about Mr. Dark, about the hooligans, about other things. The light coming in the window with its Eastern exposure was deep orange and fiery red.

16

A loud noise. At first he thought it was a car racking off, but then he felt his body being shaken, and he looked up. Mr. Dark.

"Rise, shine, son. Rise, shine."

"What?"

"Rise."

"Uh, yes. Yes, I will."

He tried to, but Mr. Dark's finger was poking him in the forehead.

"Get up."

"Yes, sir. Mr. Dark."

"It's time we moved forward on this thing." He was sticking that .38 in his coat pocket. "Now... my son is the man. Of course where did he learn it from? Yours truly. I taught him everything I know. The wife didn't go for that. That's women. But you don't let women run your life. I suppose you noticed how she camped out in that hospital when he was in a coma. You think that was wise? They know things when they're in a coma. Maybe you don't think they do, but they do. Yes, they do."

"What? Know what?"

"More than you'd guess. That's the case. You think that boy would come out of that coma with his mother stroking his hair like he was a little child?'

"I don't know. Didn't he?"

"Yes, he did. Once I threw her out of the room. Well, not actually. Not physically. Well, close to it. I wouldn't have that sort of thing. You've got to be tough. Tough love is what it's all about. You don't know, I don't know, he didn't know—who does know? We're stuck with the hand we're dealt. Live it, love it. A bitch, but that's what it is. You think I don't know that? Huh?"

"No. I guess. I guess."

"You guess what?"

"Well, I guess you did and do know what."

"And that is?"

"Uh, I don't know."

"No, you don't because you're a pansy ass, aren't you? But you carry a piece like I've got on me, and that evens things up. More than a little. A man who carries a piece— an equalizer, as it were—such a man's not a pansy ass."

"No."

"No, what?"

"No, Mr. Dark."

"Now, then, are you ready? Are you equipped to go after those hooligans?"

"I... don't know. I need some sort of... weapon or something."

"Sure you do. And I know just what it is."

The man beckoned him to follow.

He followed Mr. Dark into the kitchen.

The man went for a drawer. He rummaged around with metal noises. Then he came forth with a long screwdriver.

A flat edge one, the metal glinting. It was the longest screwdriver Frederick had ever seen.

"I filed it down a bit—see?"

It was right in Frederick's face. He backed off a little.

Mr. Dark thrashed it in the air.

"Yes, sir."

"Take it, then," said Mr. Dark.

He did. But where to put it?

"Pocket," said Mr. Dark. "Coat pocket."

The man marched toward the front room. He grabbed Frederick's coat off the couch. He slung it at him.

Frederick got it on. He got the long screwdriver in it.

"Um," he said.

Mr. Dark stared at him. "And now we're off. No, we're not going to eat first. That'll weaken us. We're going straight to that place you marked on your map, such as it is. That's where we're going, and we'll catch something out there as we interrogate the help. Ready?"

"Yes, sir. Mr. Dark."

※ ※ ※

Mr. Dark accompanied him to a Lexus, one hand gripping his shoulder.

"In the back," said Mr. Dark, pointing.

Frederick started to get in the front.

"The back!"

"Yes, sir. Mr. Dark."

The car was now moving. He carefully removed the screwdriver and stuck it under the floor mat.

From where he sat, he could observe the speedometer. He watched and mentally noted the speeds. Mr. Dark drove sixty over the roads leading to the interstate, hit eighty on the interstate, ramped it up to ninety, and whizzed by a trooper. But the trooper didn't do a thing. He thought he caught a hand waving.

"Why? How?" said Frederick. "Why'd he—"

In the rearview mirror, he could see the man's mouth grotesquely stretched over long, narrow teeth. "One of my very own, son. Just one. He's not the only one."

"He waved. Didn't he?"

"You're very observant."

A bit later, Mr. Dark whammed the Lexus into the bumpy lot of the Bronco Motel and Steakhouse. He got out. Frederick got out.

Mr. Dark headed for the steakhouse, with Frederick on his heels.

Inside, Mr. Dark looked about. Then he headed to a booth to the very back. Frederick followed. Mr. Dark sat down and Frederick sat down. There were no other customers, except on the other side of the café, a man with a long white beard, and he seemed to be fuming over something.

Frederick couldn't help but look. There were interesting gyrations. The man was mouthing something at no apparent person. Then his middle finger shot up, and he was looking straight at Frederick.

"What the?" said Frederick. "What the?"

"Oh, him," said Mr. Dark. "Takes all kinds."

"Yeah, but—"

"What?"

"We going to let him sit there like that and shoot the bird at us?"

"Um. Well, sir, we could go over and allow him to know... I suppose we could do that."

"Know. Know what?"

"That he'll be doing a long stay in ICU if he keeps it up."

"But he's an old man. Surely you wouldn't, surely—"

Mr. Dark raised a finger, a remonstrative one, "Let me inform you, son, that there are givers and there are takers. That man is a taker; I'm a giver. On the other hand, right now that man is a giver, and I'm a taker."

"What am I?"

"There's no telling."

The white-bearded man still had that middle finger up.

"What is his problem?" said Frederick.

"I suppose he's unhappy and he wants everyone to be as unhappy as he is. But we can't fix that, can we? Read your Mill."

"Huh?"

"John Stuart."

"Oh."

"But we can fix him, now can't we?" He rose from the table.

"Wait a minute," said Frederick. "You're not going over there, are you?"

"Momentarily. Yes."

"What if it's some sort of ailment—like he broke his finger?"

"Too bad, eh?"

"Well, I—I should go too."

"If you think you're man enough."

Frederick rose. He wasn't sure. He wanted to be. He hated that middle finger, which persisted in being straight up. And the man's eyes were right on them. Though as Mr. Dark made his way over to the white-bearded man, the man's eyes shifted toward this mobster. And the middle finger—it stayed straight up.

Frederick started for that table. He would not be left alone to observe the proceedings of what—who could know what?

But suddenly the white-bearded man hurled his plate directly at Mr. Dark, who somehow side-stepped it, like a graceful dance step, and moved toward that man with the white beard and middle finger.

Frederick stopped. He couldn't seem to move.

The man with the white beard yelled, "Come on, come on, son!"

Mr. Dark pulled his pistol. He rammed it in that white beard. The man's middle finger dropped, and he grinned.

"Go ahead," he shouted. "Shoot. I'd love it. Wouldn't you, Elinor?"

Frederick saw the lady with the apron heading toward Mr. Dark and the man with the white beard.

"No need for guns this morning," she said. "Take your table, sir—I'll need to get your order."

The man with the white beard said, "Hell, yes, there is. This man wants to get his shot in. Go ahead. Blow my head off."

Mr. Dark withdrew his pistol and pocketed it. Then he sat down across from the man with the white beard, and they started talking, but Frederick couldn't hear them.

They were laughing over something.

The man in the white beard was lighting up. Blowing smoke.

Mr. Dark was waving his hand at the smoke.

Soon the waitress was getting Mr. Dark's order. Mr. Dark and that white-bearded man seemed to be getting along just fine, except for that smoke, which the white-bearded man was blowing and, because of it, Mr. Dark kept waving his hand.

Suddenly Mr. Dark pulled that pistol and rammed it against the white-bearded man's forehead.

The white-bearded man snuffed out his cigarette, and Mr. Dark pocketed his pistol.

The waitress then showed up at Frederick's table.

✿ ✿ ✿

Frederick ate, observing the two of them, Mr. Dark and that white-bearded man. He drank coffee.

Thirty minutes later, Mr. Dark was heading to the front of the restaurant.

Frederick quickly followed him

"What about paying?"

"Forget it."

Frederick looked back at the white-bearded man. No

middle finger raised. But he had a grim grin on his face, and he was licking his thick, rubbery lips.

"Out there, that's where we're headed." Mr. Dark grabbed Frederick by the shoulder. "Now then, we'll see, won't we?"

"What? See what?"

"What we see."

Outside, the sun was up. It was a red blotch in a pale white sky. Frederick took a blow right across the chops. He fell backward against the building. And then another bouncing his head against the door, and then another and still another.

"What the?" yelled Frederick.

"Now, then, are you coming to understand?" said Mr. Dark.

"Understand... what?"

He wiped his lips with a tentative finger. Bloody.

He was grabbed by the shirt collar. He was face to face with Mr. Dark, who wore a nasty grin, nastier than the white-bearded man's. He was showing teeth, sharp dog-like teeth. He looked like he might bite, savagely.

Frederick shoved him. He shoved, and then he struck out. He connected one right on Mr. Dark's chin. He felt, heard bones snap. The man fell back. He started to regain his balance, but Frederick hit him again, then again, and still again.

This wasn't him doing it. It was something pushing him. It was like the pummeling he'd given Mr. Dark's son. Only that wasn't a pummeling. It was one fist against one chin, one time. This was a true pummeling. He took some pride in it.

"What the?" shouted Mr. Dark, rubbing his chin. "Now that's performance! That'll do! When those hooligans show, that's what you do. See? That's what that man in there with the white beard said to do. He ought to know. He's their grandpa."

"Grandpa?"

"That's right."

"He wants me to beat them up?"

"Most assuredly, he does. He said, and now listen, if you don't beat them up, he'll beat you up. He don't like sissies. He saw you. He saw you with that phone of yours inside there, talking. Calling 911, weren't you?"

"Yes, sir."

"Mr. Dark."

"Mr. Dark."

Slap across the face. Hard. "Cowardly," said Mr. Dark.

"Ow!"

"No cops." Mr. Dark suddenly had a nasal twang, and this confused Frederick.

"Why was he giving us the finger?"

"Not us—you."

"He gave it to you, too."

"Because of you. Well, now, I've got some good things in my trunk. So let's go see."

Frederick followed Mr. Dark out to his car. The man clicked his remote and then went for the trunk. An assembly of ball bats lay about.

"The only thing worse than a hooligan is a mobster with a bat. Here, take one. Here, take three or four."

He grabbed two. His stomach took a dive.

Mr. Dark grabbed three, slammed the trunk lid shut, and made his way to the front of the car.

"I don't see them," said Frederick. He didn't hear them either.

"They'll show. Patience, son."

And then he heard it. He heard the wheeze of a car, like an advanced bronchial infection, and the cackling of discordant voices, and he saw the maroon car ramming it hard, banging pot holes, leaping up, banging down, then skidding sideways into the lot.

It pulled up to a sudden stop and then sat there, the

motor racing.

And then all five of the young hooligans got out, each of them swinging a tire iron.

What he saw next was Mr. Dark with three bats, heading into the fray. Then he himself was running into the steakhouse and seeing the white-bearded man with that middle finger shooting up.

He had 911 on the phone, but suddenly the old man was right there in his face, upon him.

❧ ❧ ❧

He awoke to a bad headache, with blurry vision. He was on the floor with Mr. Dark looking down at him. The man was shaking his head.

"Up, son, that'll do."

He didn't answer. He couldn't answer.

"You got it in the head. But look at me."

Mr. Dark's forehead looked caved-in, but maybe it wasn't. Maybe that was just the blood; but no, it was caved in.

"Metal plate's in there," said Mr. Dark. "It was at a sitdown, but that's another story." He dabbed it with a handkerchief, only it was still bleeding. It was bleeding sort of bad.

"You need... medical attention."

"No. They do."

"What?"

"Up, son."

"Uh. Ugh."

Mr. Dark pulled him up, to a standing position. He pointed to several bodies out in the lot. They were piled on each other the way he'd seen bodies piled in pictures of the Civil War dead—in History class.

"Are they... are they dead?"

Mr. Dark shrugged. "Don't know. Don't care. But they could be. That'd be a shame, now wouldn't it?"

"What are we going to do?"

"Leave them there, of course."

"But they'll get run over."

"That's not so bad. Worse things happen to people. There are terrible things I could tell you about, son. Just terrible, but we'll save that for another day."

"What about the cops?"

"Cops?"

"Shouldn't we report it?"

"Naw."

"Where's my cell phone?"

"Smashed. See that?"

He saw. To one side of the door. Stomped on, metal parts littered about.

"There was money in that car, son. You'll get your share. Let's move on now."

And then Frederick looked to that table in the café. There sat the white-bearded man with his middle finger up.

❧ ❧ ❧

Mr. Dark dropped him off at his apartment.

"Know this, son. They'll be back. And they'll find both of us. I assure you."

Mr. Dark handed him a stash of dollars.

He started to count it.

"Eighty. Out now."

He pocketed it.

Frederick got out just as Mr. Dark headed off in his Lexus. He made the stairs.

The light was on, inside.

17

"**W**hat? What?"

"You think you can ditch me like that? Where have you been?"

"Out. How'd you get in?"

"I just did. Where?"

He didn't want to tell her about Ginger from the payday loans place. He didn't want to tell her about the judge or the lawyer, or Mr. Dark. But he sat down and hoped he didn't hear rats. Or hoped she didn't.

"You got another girl or something?"

"No. No I don't."

"You don't sound very convincing."

"I don't?"

"What's her name?"

He wasn't going to say it. Besides, how was Ginger his girlfriend? He had taken just one trip out to the impoundment lot with her, one trip to her ex-boyfriend's house, and had his car towed out to a body shop. Was that cheating on Lilac? Yet he felt guilty because he'd been turned on by that Ginger. That'd have to count, wouldn't it?

"No name."

"I'm pregnant—is that why you're dumping me?"

He looked at her middle. But he couldn't decide. She didn't look pregnant.

"Quit that."

"Oh, sorry."

"Don't be sorry."

"I won't."

"You'd better. Look, you going to marry me or not?"

"I will. I think."

"You'd best know. My father has connections. He could have you thrown in jail."

"For what?"

"For clobbering that poor Dork."

"Dark. But the judge is satisfied about that. No hearing. Cancelled."

"My father could get that all opened up again. The judge is putty in his hands."

"He wants me to marry you?"

"He wants someone to marry me."

"And you?"

"If we're married, it doesn't mean you can take liberties with me. That's not part of the deal."

"Huh? What?"

"Oh, so you thought—you would think like that, being a man. Or a boy, really. You're not really a man. I want a man. Not a boy."

"Why then would any man, or boy, marry you? If he couldn't—"

"Say it. Achieve coitus?"

"Yes..."

"Well because maybe someday he could. He could hope anyway."

"I'm not marrying you, then," he said. "Not like that."

"You know Dork was going to marry me? Thought he

was, anyway. I told him a big no, though, and that's why he called me a bitch. You were good to flatten him. That was good. But you did know, didn't you, that the judge is related to the Darks—on his mother's side. She's gone, of course. In her coffin a bunch of years."

"How, then, how—"

"Conflict of interest?"

"Yes."

"That doesn't bother the judge at all." She beckoned him to come to the bed. She patted a place on the bed.

He lay down.

"Now, then, we could pretend, and I'll let you know."

He heard those noises again.

"Rats!" she yelled. "Rats!"

She was up in a flash and at the door. He heard clomp noises on the steps, and then there she was, the landlady, right on the landing, sticking her head in.

"You two sleeping together, are you? Well, I won't have it!"

He wanted to say he hadn't had a minute of trying yet, but how could he say that?

"I'm never coming back!" shouted Lilac. "You and your rats!"

"Rats?" said the landlady. "There's no rats in my house!"

But Lilac was running out to her car at that point. He shoved by the landlady, locked his door, and he yelled at Lilac, just as she was about to get in her car, "I need a ride!"

"What? Where to?"

"To get my car."

"Where is it?"

"Body shop."

"You might as well buy a new one."

"No, no."

"That'll never fix. Jeez."

❧ ❧ ❧

And now they were speeding out to the body shop, though he couldn't remember exactly where it was.

"You tell me where the place is, please," said Lilac.

He told her. As best he could.

"Well, where is that?"

He told her that too. As best he could.

And they were there in about twenty minutes, pulling into the lot. No red car here. He looked about. No, none.

"I've got to use the restroom," he said.

"Oh, god. Please. You think I want to sit here, a sitting duck?"

"For what?"

"Use your brain."

"Oh," he said. "Well, I'll be right out."

In there he called the payday loan place and asked for Ginger. Her voice came on, and he immediately wondered why he was with Lilac Johnson instead of her.

He wondered where, in hell, her boyfriend had towed his car. He couldn't remember, couldn't get a fix on that. And then he realized he shouldn't have said "hell."

"Well, that's nice," she said. "Where have you been anyway?"

"Out and about," he said. And he again asked her for the name of the place and the location.

"If you'll be nice to me, I'll tell you," she said. "But you'd better be nice."

He said he was coming in to see about another loan and he'd see her then, and he'd be in that red car, which he was planning on getting all fixed up—somehow. And nice. "You bet. It's a beauty when it's not all beat up," he said. "And so are you."

Ooh, he didn't mean that.

"He doesn't hit me anymore," she said. "Does it show?"

"No, no. I just—I'm taking you for a big ride!" he half shouted.

"Really?"

"The wind in your hair."

"Oh, I like that," she said.

And then he asked again—the name and the location, so he could get that car all fixed up for her. Somehow. If she knew what he meant.

"Oh, I do," she said. And she said it was YOUR TOTAL BODY SHOP. And it was on Masters Drive right before you got on the interstate.

"Thanks," he said.

"Is that all I get?"

"I'd kiss you," he said. "If I could."

"Um," she said and made kissing noises. In that loan place. But it sounded good to him, and he was feeling pretty high when he returned to Lilac's car.

"What are you grinning about?"

"I found out the place."

"Yeah? How'd you find that out?"

"It's where the tow truck driver said it was, and I'd forgotten."

That could have been true, he thought, though it wasn't.

"Well, you have me drive all over town. Okay, let's go."

And they did. They ended up at YOUR TOTAL BODY SHOP just as a guy was pulling down the garage door.

Frederick got out of the car and hurried toward him. He said how his was the red car over there, the badly beaten one, and he wanted it fixed—totally.

"That's what we do," said the man. "That's exactly what we do." He went over to it, off to the side of the lot. There it was looking forlorn like it had been totally battered and junked. It had been battered and junked. He felt sorry for it. No one should ever do that to a car.

"How much—would you say?" said Frederick.

"Oh, off hand... off hand, well, I'm going to say, well... minimum thirty-five thousand. Considering how this is an expensive car with expensive parts, it could go to forty. Not much over that, though. I'll give you a real estimate tomorrow if you want—if you have that kind of cash."

"That's a terrible, awful... lot of money," said Frederick.

He saw Lilac fidgeting in her car, motioning with her hands out the window, and so he said he'd call tomorrow, and he was soon back in the car.

She dropped him off at his apartment, but even though he pleaded with her to come up because he desperately needed company, just now, having seen that beaten-up car, she shook her head. "No. No. Get a better place."

They lingered in the car.

"I will."

"When?"

"Those aren't rats."

"Yes, they are."

"They sound like rats, but they're not rats. Not really."

"Well, if you want me to sleep with you, it's not going to be there. That's for sure."

That's when he wanted to know if a motel would be okay.

"No!"

"Why not?"

"Because I said so."

"Oh."

"I'm pregnant," she said. "You keep forgetting. You might hurt me."

"Oh, no," he said. "I wouldn't."

"How do you know?"

"You're not that pregnant."

"How do you know? What do you know about it?"

"Nothing, but—"

"Sure, sure, if that's what you want, but I'll hate you."

"No, no," he said.

"If we're going to get married. If that's where this is going," she said.

"We are?"

"Unless I go to one of those places where they do that stuff in a stealthy way—you know what I'm getting at?"

"Yes."

"I'll bet you don't. Well, I'll just give it up, whatever it is. Boy, girl, whatever."

"That boyfriend of yours," he said.

"You leave him alone. You don't say a word about him. Not one."

"Okay."

"Not one. You don't know a thing about him. I loved him, whatever you think."

"You still do?"

"I don't know."

"You don't?"

"He was special."

She looked like she might start sobbing, so he let up. He didn't want a girl to start sobbing.

"You want a drink?" he asked.

"Like what?"

"Bourbon?"

"No. Scotch."

"I don't have Scotch. But I do have bourbon, and I have brandy."

"I'll take that."

"Okay," he said.

"I'm not supposed to be drinking," she said. "In my condition."

She got out of the car. They went up.

❧ ❧ ❧

Drinking. Drinking. Up there in that dumpy little place of his. She was right—it was.

Sex? It was so little, he thought. Nothing was showing at all. What could it hurt?

She was half lit when he tried to make a move on her, but half lit, she got angry. "You think you can seduce me with that brew of yours?"

"No."

"Yes, you do."

"You're not in the mood?"

"No. I'm going home now."

"Can I... can I go with you?"

"To my home?"

"Yes."

"No. Of course not!"

"I'm getting that apartment," he said. "In a few days."

She was standing, but she sat back down. "Where?"

He made it up. A place he knew close to the college campus halfway across town.

"Oh, that's really nice. That place is. How much?"

A number came to him. He said it.

"Oh, god, that's a lot. How are you coming up with all that?"

"I got a job. That's how."

"Um. Where?"

He told her. How he'd started with a reputable attorney. How it looked promising. How he was going into pre-law.

"Well, hell," she said. "That's nice."

And then she lay down on the bed. He lay down with her. But when he went for her jeans to try to pull them down, she slapped him. "Don't ruin it!"

"Oh, sorry," he said.

"Don't be sorry. I hate sorry."

"Okay."

"Don't say that."

"What do you want me to say?"

"I hate everything. Everything. Why do I have to be knocked-up?"

He wanted to say because, because you had sex with that boyfriend of yours, and that's what happens. It's natural. Millions of sperms. One's bound to fertilize the egg. That's the way it works. They talked that up big in Biology.

But he didn't say anything. He looked at her and then away from her.

"You don't have anything comforting to say to me? At all?"

He paused. Then: "Sure. We'll get married and we'll have that one, plus more."

"Oh go to hell!"

"Huh?"

"I'm leaving. When you get that apartment, call me. Or text me. But not before."

He watched her leave. On the landing, he watched her get in her car. He watched it snort off. Loud.

18

The next afternoon he made his way on foot all the way out to the body shop. No, he didn't have insurance.

"Thirty-one thousand and five hundred," the man said.

"And that's rounding it down a little."

"Would you take a down and a little every month?"

"No."

"How about the windows only?" he said.

"Let's go inside and we'll see," said the body man.

"Okay."

It was about ten minutes. The body man slid a slip of paper to him. "They don't give these away, you know."

Twelve hundred and seventy-five.

"Um," he said.

"I'll have to take it as it is," said Frederick.

"Then I'd best tape it up—at least," said the body man. "You're not driving it off like that. Probably call for some cardboard, too."

It was a half hour or so.

When Frederick went for his billfold, the man said, "It's a pitiful thing. Don't bother. It's on me."

❦ ❦ ❦

Ginger wasn't there. He could see that right off. But another girl was running the show, and she was even prettier. He saw her name tag: Lexie.

He wanted to ask about borrowing more, but she directed him to the line of chairs. "You'll have to wait, sir," she said. "Right there with the rest of them."

"I'll wait." He asked about Ginger.

"Her? She's no longer with us."

"Oh, no," he said. "She was just..."

"Why? What's it to you?"

"I... she was sure nice."

"Well, we didn't think so."

"Oh?"

"You sit down and wait. All right?"

"Yes, ma'am."

She gave him a look. She blew on her red nails.

❦ ❦ ❦

He waited three hours.

Finally, the new woman, who looked better and better the more he studied her, signaled him. The man in the red shirt was back there, and he was to go to the man in the red shirt, just as before.

"I want to borrow more," said Frederick, taking a seat. He supplied his name.

The man in the red shirt looked at his computer. "Um," he said.

"What?"

"Um."

"What?"

"Well, now, right now, you're up to four thousand, three

hundred, fifty-seven dollars, and thirty-three cents. That's what you owe—at this point."

"What?"

"Takes in interest compounded, plus several fees, plus minimum charges, including insurance, disability—all kinds of stuff. A bit boring, let me tell you, to rehearse such stuff and all the details in the contract, but there we go. If you pay now, it's the amount I just gave you. If you pay an hour from now, it's more. Not a whole lot more, but more. Ten, fifteen bucks—who knows? Could be thirty, forty."

"I don't want to pay. I want to borrow—more."

"Um."

"Huh?"

"Not happening, sir."

Frederick couldn't help but watch that girl Lexie.

"She's a looker, isn't she?"

"Pardon?"

The guy in the red shirt pointed. "Out of your league, son."

"Why? Why do you say that?"

"Got a boyfriend. A hunk of a guy. Six-five. Two twenty-five. Male model. Lots of gigs. Any guy even looks at her, he puts them in the hospital. Out at that bar. She goes out there with him. If he says to step outside, you're dead meat. One punch from that guy, it's curtains, as they say."

"What kind of car does the guy drive?"

"Fancy."

"But what?"

"Corvette. Ferrari."

"Damn."

"Forget it."

"How old is he?"

"Older than you."

"How old, though."

"Thirty, thirty-one, thirty-two, I don't know."

"Damn," he said.

"Yeah," said the man in the red shirt. "Look I've agonized and agonized for a full day now. You know what it's like sitting back here watching that bottom of hers wiggling around? You know what it's like sitting here watching that sensual hair she tosses about? You know what it's like sitting here and watching those boobs spilling out of that skimpy white blouse she's sporting? Huh, you think I haven't about cashed it in watching all that? I'm a miserable man, son. When a man has needs, he must have them taken care of. I've got needs. But you think she'd give me a second glance? No. And you? Ha! You think you can stack up to that brute who wheels her around in that silver Ferrari? That red corvette? Ha!"

"Red?"

"As a tomato."

"What do we do?" said Frederick.

"Just try to put her out of your mind. Only if you're sitting back here, you can't. But if you're you, you just make it out of here as fast as your shoes will go and don't look back. Don't give her one look. That's where you'd go wrong. Seriously wrong."

"Okay," said Frederick. "But I need to borrow more. What can you do? What can you do for me?"

"Pay off what you owe, and we'll see."

Frederick rose from his plastic chair. He shook the hand of the man in the red shirt. Then he made his way to the front.

Suddenly, a voice, a female voice: "Come back now."

He shot her a look. Oh, god. "Okay," he said.

"Don't be a stranger," she said.

19

He was back to Bulge's office after a full day at school. But that wouldn't last long. He was to graduate in May unless he had to go to summer school. Right now, he had some money to work off—those advances. "You ought to know," said Bulge, "that your fate isn't going to be a pleasant one if you ignore certain obligations."

"Everything we do, or don't do, shapes our future."

"Yes, sir."

"We must say yes to it whatever it is. It's we who have shaped it. No one else. And even if we haven't shaped it, well... "

"But those hooligans," said Frederick.

"Ah," said Bulge. "Yes."

"What?"

"Files, files—get to them."

He wanted to quit. But he couldn't because he owed Bulge too much..

✻ ✻ ✻

After he got off work, he took a taxi to the apartment group. Posh. Well, not exactly posh, but it was if you were thinking about that cramped room above the landlady's rat-infested ceiling. Gray brick siding. He wanted it

"Come," said the manager. "I'll show you an apartment." He was looking at him in an odd way. What was it about those lips? They looked too tight over his teeth.

In minutes he'd made up his mind. This was enough, along with that red car, to attract Lilac, Ginger, and that new girl, in spite of that vicious, tough guy she was going with. Only that brutal bruiser had a better red car than his. Or he assumed he did. Perhaps after he'd repaired it, he should trade up for an even better one.

Two bedrooms. Unfurnished, though. Still, he'd get some cheap furniture. Not too cheap, though.

"I want it. I'm sold."

"Fifteen hundred a month," said the manager. "First month, last month, plus a deposit. Comes to forty-five hundred. Plus, we'll have to run a background check. Are you at least eighteen?"

"You bet."

"Well, if you're not, we'll find that out soon enough."

It wasn't fair. He'd have to get Bulge to rent it for him. Somehow. After all, he was trying to turn his life around, forsake his criminal past. Wasn't he? Bulge worked around the clock. He must be fixed for money.

❧ ❧ ❧

At Bulge's, he went over Mr. Dark's baseball bats. He went over the drug money—his eighty bucks. He went over it all.

"Then you stole it. That eighty dollars?"

"No. Mr. Dark did."

"Just an accomplice, huh?"

"Well."

"You think that's the whole kit and caboodle?"

"Huh?"

"What makes you think so?"

"That's what Mr. Dark gave me."

Bulge laughed. It was a loud cackle. "You trust a man like that? He's skinning you, son. Probably smalltime stuff, but still... if after a drug deal, who knows? Mr. Dark's a bigger mobster than they are. He probably walked off with a bunch of dough."

"A bunch?"

"A bunch, son. Don't be a fool. You make sure you get the rest of what's coming to you."

He brought up the apartment. Would Bulge help?

That loud cackle again? "No, no. No. You get Mr. Dark to do that. They won't even ask for a background check. You think they're going to rile a man like Mr. Dark? Or better yet, his son?"

"Ask his son?"

"No, no, don't do that."

"Mr. Dark."

"That's what I said."

20

He stood before Mr. Dark. Back in that room where there were two more rooms to go through to get to the front entrance. It was late evening, and the room seemed to be cast in shadows. An orange sun grew angry through one uncurtained window.

When he told Mr. Dark about the apartment, he said there were three women he wanted, and without that apartment, what was he going to do—with that landlady in the picture? If the bed springs made any noise at all, if she heard them laughing and carrying on, or making noises of any kind—love noises, especially—then that landlady would run up the outside steps and she had the key too! "What am I supposed to do?" he asked. "I wanted... I wanted to ask a man of the world. I figured... I figured you as a man of the world."

Mr. Dark smirked. "The throes of young love. If you want that kind of thing, you're going to have to work for it."

"I was thinking. What about all that money from those hooligans?"

"Pardon?"

"What you must've walked off with," said Frederick. "A bunch." He didn't like the way that came out, but so be it —he must move on. He had it on good authority, he said, assuming they'd made (those hooligans, he meant) a... you know, drug deal of some sort... you know, and he wanted his cut. That's all. "Please," he whined, "I'm desperate for some money. I've got all kinds of stuff to deal with—that car, now an apartment, girls—you know."

Mr. Dark laid a hand on his shoulder. It was a fatherly hand, only then he squeezed. Too hard, he squeezed. "Is that right?"

"Yes, sir."

"Mr. Dark."

"Mr. Dark, sir."

"You've got a lot of nerve, don't you?"

He was in the inner chamber, and again Mr. Dark was standing in the doorway preventing egress.

"Well," he said. He might be able to take him. He did, after all, get some good punches in out there at the Bronco. There was no gun in the man's hand.

"It wasn't a bunch."

"How much?"

"You get it if you think you can, son."

He saw the man's black eyes. He saw the man's hands starting to clench into fists.

"No," said Frederick. "But I do need it to get those women. And what those women want—and need."

"Sure you do. And I've got some work for you. Every young man like you needs a place to take his woman. Without some old biddy interfering."

"That's right."

"There's a man I want you to deliver a package to."

"Package?"

Mr. Dark made his way over to his desk and opened a drawer. He came forth with a package wrapped in brown paper. A note was taped to the top of it. A pink-colored memo.

"Here's the package. And here's where to deliver it."

Frederick shook his head. "I'm not doing that."

Mr. Dark shoved the package at him. "Don't disappoint me, son."

Frederick held it, and then he set it down.

Mr. Dark left for a moment. Frederick bolted for the door. He got through it and out into the street. He crossed to the other side. He was in someone's front yard.

He looked back. There stood Mr. Dark. Tall, with a face chiseled out of rock, in one huge fist swinging a bat.

Frederick ran and ran.

❧ ❧ ❧

He told Mr. Bulge about it.

"What did you think he'd do? Just hand you a pile of money? A man like that makes deals. They've got to be to his advantage. He cuts people out, not in—every chance he gets."

"What do you think was in that package?"

"Let's don't think about that. You never want to think about a thing like that."

"What am I to do?"

"You'll have to give up the apartment."

"No!"

"What else but that?"

❧ ❧ ❧

He drove straight to Lilac Johnson's. He got out, slammed the door. Took off. He tried not to look at that mangled mess of a car of his.

He made it up the sidewalk to the door.

He knocked three times. Then waited. He knocked three more times. Then waited. He knocked three more times.

There she stood at the door, Lilac in blue jeans and

tank top. Wasn't her stomach protruding just a little?

"Did you get that apartment yet?" She looked out at the car. "When're you going to fix that?"

He went on in. "I don't have the money for either."

"Maybe you can borrow it."

"I can't, and I'm not eighteen anyway." He spotted a sofa and sat there, then motioned for her.

"Why not?"

"Huh?"

"Why aren't you?"

"Eighteen?"

"Yes—eighteen!"

"I'm just not."

"Well, hell. When will you be?"

"August."

"August!"

"Yes."

"Well, I'm not going to that dump of an apartment you've got. I'm not doing that. You get that apartment, that decent, actual apartment, or you can just forget me."

"Oh, please," he cried, taking her into his arms. "I can't. Ever."

"Well, that's the way it is. No girl wants to go to a place like that."

"It's all mine," he said. "It's not my father's place."

"What's that like?"

"Huh?"

"Is it private—at all?"

"No." But then he said, "He's gone sometimes."

"Forget it."

"Where's your father?" he said.

"He wants me to get married. He can't stand abortions. He's old school. He can't stand adoptions. He was adopted. He can't stand single mothers. But I guess it'll just have to be the surgical route. Because I'm not living in a dump—no, sir."

"Where is he?"

"Where? How would I know?"

"I want to speak to him."

"He wants you to marry me. You know why?"

"Why?"

"Because you beat up that Dork guy."

"What was so good about that?"

"You stood up for me. He likes that."

"Don't you?"

"Sure. If it was for me. Really for me."

"It was. Why would you think I'd do it if not for you?"

"You're sweet," she said, and she moved next to him.

"I want you," he said.

"In bed?"

He hadn't meant that, but that was part of it—a big part of it, of course. "Could we?"

"If you marry me."

"Not before?"

"No."

"You're already pregnant," he said.

"Don't you think I know that?"

He thought he heard something. "That your father?"

She listened, cocking her head. "Yep."

He got up. He advanced toward Mr. Johnson. And then he whispered at him. The two of them headed for another room, with a window view of the street. He could see that red car out there with a major case of the pox. Her father directed him to take a seat in a large leather chair. He went to a bar and grabbed a glass and made clinking noises with ice. He came forward with a half-filled glass of an amber liquid. He had one for himself too.

"I'm not drinking age," said Frederick.

"Oh, don't worry. Don't worry, son."

Frederick raised the glass. He took a quick sip.

"Now, then," said Lilac's father. "What do we want?"

"Money," said Frederick. "Lots of money to get an apartment. For an apartment for me and my beloved Lilac."

"Ha! Marrying her, are we? Marrying my daughter. Well, she's seventeen—won't be eighteen till July. I could have the young man that knocked her up charged as a rapist of an underage girl. Jail bait, you know. But I thought what the heck? She's a good looking girl, and the young man said he couldn't help himself. That's the way it is with the young, you know. Hormones. Who can argue with hormones?"

"Um," said Frederick. But then he didn't say more.

"You want sex with my daughter. That's the thing here, isn't it?"

He looked at Mr. Johnson, then at the floor. "Well, uh, I... want to marry her."

"You get married to have sex, don't you?"

"Uh, yes. Sure."

"Well, then?"

"I need an apartment," said Frederick. "But I'm not eighteen yet."

Mr. Johnson sipped his drink. "Why not?"

"I need an apartment. I really do."

"Every man needs an apartment. I expect you live at home."

"Not anymore. I got an apartment, only it's a bum one."

"That's too bad. How do you mean?"

He described it. He mentioned the old biddy. He mentioned the rats—well, if they were rats. "It's not the kind of apartment you can take a girl to. I mean Lilac. She won't go there. She leaves."

"You took her there?"

"Yes. But she left."

"Don't get her pregnant now, son."

"She is already. Isn't she?"

"Anybody's guess." And then he gave Frederick a conspiratorial look. "Every man your age needs a bit of help. I know that. Who doesn't?"

"Financial," said Frederick.

"Of course, of course."

There she stood. "I'll tell you want I want. For you two to quit talking about me."

"Oh," said Mr. Johnson. "Say, how about some coffee? Does anyone want coffee?"

"I hate coffee," said Lilac.

"Yes, that's right," said Mr. Johnson. "And you?" he said to Frederick. "How do you want yours?"

"No coffee," said Frederick.

"Well, then, I guess I'm alone. On that anyway. How about a beer? Everyone want a beer?"

"Yes," said Lilac, "only I can't because of the baby. There's oh so many things I can't do because of this baby!"

"I'll marry you," said Frederick.

"So you can get in my pants?"

"Well," said Frederick.

"Uh. Well, marriage, you know—"

"I guess I could have a bunch of babies. That's what men want with women. It's always a pack of babies. No, I take it back. What they want is what makes babies. That's what they want. Oh, you bet they do."

"What I'm thinking," said her father, "is that a beer would be awfully nice. About now."

"He's underage," said Lilac. "What if he smashes up that red car of his, all drunk?"

"Um. That would be a terrible thing. Yes, it would indeed." He parted the curtains. "Very nice car. Very nice. Except for the blemishes."

"How horrible," said Lilac. "Such a waste!"

21

He sat before the apartment manager. "It will be under Roger Johnson," he said. "Mr. Roger Johnson."

"Any relation to you?"

"Father-in-law."

"So you're married. No pets now."

"No."

"No wild parties."

"No. We're a decent, law-abiding couple about to have our first," he said. It was the kind of thing he imagined an adult was supposed to say.

"And you have the deposit."

"Soon," said Frederick.

The apartment manager nodded. "Now, then, which floor do you want? As you probably noticed from the outside, we have three floors. Some folks like the upper floor, some like the lower one—some like the middle. What kind of couple are you and your wife? Lower, upper, or middle?"

"I like the top floor."

"What about your wife?"

"Top floor."

"How do you know? Did you ask her? Do you speak for her? Where is she, anyway?"

"At home."

"Where is home?"

"With her father."

"You didn't think it right to bring her here to pick out this apartment? What about that baby? What about those stairs? Stairs can be treacherous, son. Do you know that? Are you aware of that?"

"Uh, yes."

"Of course you're young. Your wife is young—is she?"

"Yes. Young and beautiful."

"Stay that way."

"Huh?"

"Someday you won't be."

"I know that."

"No, you don't. No kid your age knows that. They think they'll be young forever. But see, that's not true. You get to be middle age, you'll know it's not true. You look back and you think, 'What the hell happened?'"

"I know," said Frederick.

"No, you don't. But whatever, let me give you some advice. If you're willing to hear it."

"Yes, sir."

"Sure you are."

"I am."

"Amor fati, son. Amor fati."

"What the?"

"Hell?"

"Yes, sir."

"Amor fati, son. Love your fate."

"Okay."

The man leaned toward him. Close up. Like a drill sergeant. "What's that mean? 'Okay'?"

"It means—"

"Look here, let's settle up. Your cash. Your rental

agreement. Your this, your that. Let's go over the terms of your lease. Shall we?"

"Yes, sir."

❦ ❦ ❦

He got her to go. He hurried around to the passenger side, took her in his arms, her resisting, then not resisting, then inside they went, three floors up, him hurrying, her a bit behind him, scowling, then smiling, then shouting, "Slow up, will you?"

And so he did.

Then, there they were. Right there. The door. The key. A borrowed key. The insertion. The turning of the knob, the tumblers turning. Then him taking her up in his arms, her resisting, then not resisting, then the two of them inside and him putting her down. On the carpeted floor. Wanting her to lie there before him—but that could wait. Sure. Sure it could.

She rose. Looking around. "God," she said. "God."

"Yes," he said. "Yes."

"I don't know," she said. "I really... don't know."

"What? What don't you know?"

"Well, if the kitchen is in the right place. Right to the left of the living area. I don't know. The cooking smells, the drink glasses, the washing of dishes. Guests. I don't know."

"It'll be fine," he said. "Just fine."

She pointed toward the hallway. "One or two bed-rooms?"

"Two, I think," he said.

"You don't know?"

"Two."

"One," she said. "Just one. And no bed."

"We'll get a bed all right, you bet," he said. "I can assure you."

"Yeah, you would think of that. And me pregnant as I can be."

"But you're not—"

"I want a decent mattress. Maybe I'll bring my own. Not yours!"

"No," he said.

"God only knows what's in yours: bed bugs, lice, spiders. I shudder—"

He again took her in his arms. He wanted to, right on the carpeted floor.

She saw his design. Intention. His dream.

"No, not yet. We move in, then at that time."

"Married?" he said.

"We'll see," she said.

"See?"

"I mean I'm not sure. I'm not totally sure."

"What... what are you not sure about?"

"Well, things..."

"Like what... things?"

"Him."

"Huh? Who?"

"My boyfriend. The one who did this to me." She pointed at her abdomen. It did look slightly enlarged. Bulged out, just a little. Not a lot, just a little.

"You... you're still thinking of him?"

"Some."

He wanted to punch the guy out. He wanted to punch him out for any number of reasons, for one, getting his girlfriend, his soon-to-be wife, pregnant. Knocked up. With child. He wanted to land a punch right on the chin, just like with Horatio Dark. A mobster, a made man, a professional killer, and he'd decked the bastard. You bet he had.

"What's he to you besides 'that,'" he said, pointing. And he immediately regretted putting it that way.

Her eyes zoned in on him. "That?"

"Well, I meant—I didn't mean—"

"I suppose when we have about ten kids you'll refer to each of our offspring as That 1, That 2, That 3—isn't that right. You will, won't you?"

"Ten?" he said. "Really?"

"Figure of speech." She was standing in the half darkness of the hallway, and she suddenly looked matronly, older, like a mother thirty to forty to fifty. It scared him. He blinked twice.

"One," he said. "Two's about right. One maybe?"

"You don't want one with me?" she said. "Just this one I'm carrying?"

"I do want one with you," he said.

"How many?" Her eyebrows raised.

"Two," he said. "With you."

"That would give me three kids. My god, how could I manage three kids?"

"One," he said.

"That might do," she said, and she disappeared into the darkness of the hall. It was a long hall.

He followed.

She was peering into the bathroom. Then she was peering into the bedroom, with no furniture.

"I'll have to move my chest of drawers, my vanity, and my night table in here," she said, "with my bed."

"Pack up and leave home," he said.

"Huh?"

"What?"

"Why'd you say that?" She wheeled toward him.

"Say what?"

"Why did you say that?"

"I didn't mean... anything. I meant—"

"I'm not necessarily doing this," she said. "It still remains to be seen if I'm doing this."

"But your father... I'm hoping..."

"Him? Ha!"

"What?"

"You think he'll help you—us? Ha!"

"But..."

"And me? You have it all worked out, don't you? But what about me? Maybe I have a different idea about my life. And it might not be the same as yours."

"Like what?"

"Oh, well. Oh, God. Like leaving the country, sticking the kid in some orphan's home, blowing a bunch on my father's charge cards—who knows? I sure don't intend to be your little woman going to the park with my perambulator to watch my little ones on the playground equipment."

"Per—what?" he said.

"I suppose you don't know the word," she said.

"No," he said. He was thinking about that bed. Was it queen-sized? Cranberry bedspread, like the curtains? It wasn't a double, he was sure of that. There'd be plenty of room.

She was staring at him. "You," she said.

"What?"

"What are you thinking?"

"Of you," he said. He had to spill it, how he wanted her all naked in this room for about ten hours straight and that's all he really wanted. The kids—let them go. Who wanted kids anyway? He hinted at it. Strongly.

"You don't have to worry about that for about another seven months. After that? That depends on you."

"Me?"

"Vasectomy," she said. "Ever heard of it?"

"No," he said. "No."

"It doesn't hurt, they say."

"Who says?"

"I don't know. How am I supposed to know?"

"No," he said.

She put her finger to her lips. "Don't tell anyone, but my father is a real idiot."

"Huh?"

"My mother left him since he was such a big idiot. We lost the house twice."

"Um."

"She swooped in and saved it. But she couldn't swoop in and save him."

"She couldn't?"

"Do I stutter?"

"No."

"She's great to swoop in, but sometimes it doesn't work. My dad is the prime case of that."

"Yeah."

"What do you know of it?"

"I don't—"

"Then why did you agree?"

He moved up close to her. "On the floor," he whispered. "It'd be nice. Feel that carpet?"

"Ha! You can just forget it. Until we're married. Besides, what would my boyfriend think?"

"You still... you still."

"I still. I've got to go."

"Okay."

"You're not going to fight to save me?"

He grabbed her. He grabbed her around the waist. He swung her up and around. For a moment, he felt the palpable sensation of being an alpha male. There she was, there he was, there was this room with the thick, soft carpet, and soon, and soon.

"Damn!" she yelled. "What do you think you're doing. Besides, I'm pregnant, you know. You want to kill this living little being in me and be up for murder?"

"No, oh no," he said.

"But let's lie down," she said, and she moved to a sitting position on the floor, then to a lying one. He moved, carefully, to a sitting, then a lying, position next to her. She was then in his arms.

"This is cheap carpet," she said. "Truth be told. You think it's so fine, so elegant, because of that cheapo dive you live in. And I'll bet, I'm sure of it, that underneath this cheapo floor covering is pressed board."

She sounded like she knew the biz or something. He asked.

"I used to work in this place with all sorts of flooring. I got sick of it. I wanted to light a match." She moved to a sitting position. "You might at least help a pregnant woman up."

"Oh," he said. "Sorry."

"I suppose that's the way you'd be if we got married. You'd want to pork me, then you'd be done. Moving on and on. I'll bet you wouldn't even know how many we had." She glared at him. "Most men don't stop with one woman but go on to several. How many women do you have—right now?"

That hit him like a bolt—right in the gut. He stumbled over it. "Just you."

"Yeah, I'll bet."

He felt complimented. She thought he was attractive enough to have several. He got up, helped her up and kissed her. "Be mine," he said.

"I don't like that," she said. "I'm not anybody's. You'd have to know that. For sure."

"I do know that." But he couldn't help but think, I want her to be mine. Like on those Valentine candies. And what did that mean? It meant at least a hundred times in bed. After that, well, they'd see.

"Myself," she said, "I don't know if I could settle on one man. I don't know about that."

"Huh?" he said.

"Well," she said. "I mean it."

"Um."

"You'd have to have money, too," she said. "Plenty of it. I hate being poor. This apartment's just for starters. And fix that car!"

He looked at her for the longest time. They locked eyes.

"But how?" he said. "How?"

And then he had a vision: of those hooligans, of Mr. Dark, of that payday loan place, that car place, that judge.

"You figure it out," she said.

"Why here?" he said. "We'll go away. Far, far away."

Through the picture window, he saw it: the sun fiery red, the sky brilliant orange against a placid blue.

—END—

Acknowledgments

I want to thank the following readers of my manuscript for their favorable comments and encouragement: De-Witt Henry, Jack Remick, Walter Cummins, Mark Wish, Grant Tracey, Midge Raymond, and Christine Sneed. I especially want to thank Jack Remick for his fine introduction.

Lastly, I want to thank Kurt Lovelace, my publisher, for all his attention to this work and to the great production values.

Jack Smith

Jack Smith has an MA in creative writing and PhD in English. He has published six novels and four works of nonfiction. His most recent novels are IF WINTER COMES (2020), RUN (2020), MISS MANNERS FOR WAR CRIMINALS (2017), BEING (2016), ICON (2014), and HOG TO HOG, which won the **2007 George Garrett Fiction Prize** and was published by *Texas Review Press* in 2008.

He has published stories in numerous literary magazines, including *Southern Review, North American Review, Texas Review, Xconnect, In Posse Review,* and *Night Train.* His reviews have appeared widely in such publications as *California Review of Books, Ploughshares, Georgia Review, American Book Review, Prairie Schooner, Mid-American Review, Pleiades: Literature in Context,* the *Missouri Review,* and *Environment* magazine.

He has published several dozen articles in both *Novel & Short Story Writer's Market* and *The Writer* magazine. His creative writing book, WRITE AND REVISE FOR PUBLICATION: A 6-MONTH PLAN FOR CRAFTING AN EXCEPTIONAL NOVEL AND OTHER WORKS OF FICTION, was published in 2013 by *Writer's Digest Books*.

A collection of his articles is available in INVENTING THE WORLD: THE FICTION WRITER'S GUIDEBOOK TO CRAFT AND PROCESS. His latest nonfiction book is CONTRIBUTIONS TO LITERATURE: A TRIBUTE TO SMALL PRESS BOOKS. His coauthored nonfiction environmental book entitled KILLING ME SOFTLY was published by *Monthly Review Press* in 2002.

Besides his writing, Smith was fiction editor of *The Green Hills Literary Lantern*, an online literary magazine published by Truman State University, for 25 years.

Also by Jack Smith

Fiction

If Winter Comes
Serving House Books, 2020

Run
Serving House Books, 2020

Miss Manners for War Criminals
Serving House Books, 2017

Being
Serving House Books, 2016

Icon
Serving House Books, 2014

Hog To Hog
Texas Review Press, 2008
Winner of the 2007
George Garrett Fiction Prize

Literary Criticism

**Contributions to Literature:
A Tribute to Small Press Books**
Serving House Books, 2021

Creative Writing Books

WRITE AND REVISE FOR
PUBLICATION: A 6-MONTH
PLAN FOR CRAFTING AN EXCEPTIONAL NOVEL
AND OTHER WORKS OF FICTION
Writer's Digest Books, 2013

INVENTING THE WORLD: THE FICTION WRITER'S
GUIDEBOOK TO CRAFT AND PROCESS
Serving House Books, 2018

www.ingramcontent.com/pod-product-compliance
Lightning Source LLC
Chambersburg PA
CBHW021727190726
48289CB00008B/2721